THE PINK PUPPET

THE PINK PUPPET

A BOOK OF TALES

Robert Hilles

Library and Archives Canada Cataloguing in Publication

Title: The pink puppet : a book of tales / Robert Hilles.

Names: Hilles, Robert, author.

Identifiers: Canadiana (print) 20230150659 |
            Canadiana (ebook) 20230150675 |

ISBN 9781771616966 (softcover) | ISBN 9781771616973 (PDF) |
ISBN 9781771616997 (Kindle) | ISBN 9781771616980 (EPUB)

Classification: LCC PS8565.I48 P56 2023 | DDC C813/.54—dc23

Published by Mosaic Press, Oakville, Ontario, Canada, 2023.

MOSAIC PRESS, Publishers
www.Mosaic-Press.com
Copyright © Robert Hilles 2023

Printed and bound in Canada.

ONTARIO ARTS COUNCIL
CONSEIL DES ARTS DE L'ONTARIO
an Ontario government agency
un organisme du gouvernement de l'Ontario

Funded by the Government of Canada
Financé par le gouvernement du Canada

Canada

ONTARIO CREATES

MOSAIC PRESS
1252 Speers Road, Units 1 & 2, Oakville, Ontario, L6L 5N9
(905) 825-2130 • info@mosaic-press.com • www.mosaic-press.com

BOOKS BY ROBERT HILLES

POETRY
Look the Lovely Animal Speaks (1980)
The Surprise Element (1982)
An Angel in the Works (1983)
Outlasting the Landscape (1989)
Finding the Lights On (1991)
A Breath at a Time (1991)
Cantos from a Small Room (1993)
Nothing Vanishes (1996)
Breathing Distance (1997)
Somewhere Between Obstacles and Pleasure (1999)
Higher Ground (2001)
Wrapped Within Again: New and Selected (2003)
Slow Ascent (2005)
Partake (2010)
Time Lapse (2012)
Line (2018)
Shimmer (2019)
From God's Angle (2021)

FICTION
Raising of Voices (1993)
Near Morning (1995)
A Gradual Ruin (2004)
Don't Hang Your Soul on That (2021)
The Pink Puppet

NON-FICTION
Kissing the Smoke (1997)
Calling the Wild (2006)

Again for my wife Rain Hilles with all my love.

For Austin, Breanne, Kyle, Elizabeth, and Charlotte.

And as well to my sister Cathi and her husband Robert and their two sons: Camille and Ben. And to all my cousins and friends.

Table of Contents

Tale of:

The Tales

Tale of the Pink Puppet

THE FRONT DOOR OPENS RIGHT INTO THE LIVING ROOM. A FOX SITS in a rocking chair. Squirrels play the piano. All of this isn't visible from the street. He stands just inside the door.

Sense that? The fox asks for it can speak. In fact, the fox belongs more in this house than the man at the door. The man wears leather boots and has opened the door without knocking. He assumes this is his house.

Sense what? he asks.

That the fox says.

Okay, the man says and considers going back outside and closing the door and then opening it again and trying a second time. He knows by now that often does the trick.

Don't do that. The fox says.

Why not?

Hear that rain? Hear the river? Hear all that water? That is your doing. Why you are here now inside this house.

This isn't my house?

No. It was never your house, the fox says and gets up from the chair and shakes the man's hand because he is the kind of fox that can do that. There is much that this fox can do that most foxes can't do.

How is that possible? the man asks.

It just is, the fox says. *Now let's go to the piano and later we'll turn off that water. It is the water that brought you here. You had the sensation that you must turn it off. We must shoo the squirrels away from the piano. Then we will sit. Out the window in front of the piano there is such a view. There is much you and I need to discuss.*

The man takes off his hat and coat and joins the fox at the piano which is now quiet. The squirrels are already gone. The fox can play the piano beautifully and at first the man just watches and listens, and then in time he finds his place in the music and puts his hands to the keys and he too plays beautifully. *This is not music?*

He says and wishes to weep.

No, it isn't, the fox says. *It is the ribbon inside your soul coming loose. Wait a moment more, play a bit more, and then when you leave, all of this can go with you, even me.*

Tale of the Blue Bicycle

SHE OWNS A BLUE BICYCLE AND RIDES IT TO WORK EVERY DAY. SHE also rides it to visit friends and to go shopping for groceries. Today it's raining as she rides to work. She stops at a red light and a car pulls up beside her and the passenger window rolls down and a boy pops his head out and says, *You're wet.*

Then she hears, *Bobby,* and the window rolls up again. The boy is right she is wet, but she lives in a part of the world where the rain is warm and refreshing. At the next light a large half-ton truck pulls up beside her. It's silver and has tinted windows and she can't see inside so glances only once in that direction. When she does the engine revs.

The light turns green the truck hurries away from her and she takes her time pedaling. In time she speeds up again and the views on either side of her change. On one side is a mountain range with a fir forest greening the base of it. On the other side is the Pacific Ocean the air salty and thick and the more she pedals the more she tastes salt.

In time, she is no longer here. Not in any creepy way or due to harm or any mishap. Also, there is no blue bicycle except that it best depicts her soul or what she thinks of as the soul every living being has. She has ridden her soul and believed it carried her like a blue bicycle. She houses it and transports it as she imagines it transporting her now.

She takes her hands off the handlebars and lets the bicycle coast as though down a hill, except she is on the flat. Still, it coasts and goes on coasting as long as she holds her arms out like that buoyed on the air, and in time she is lifted and realizes that there is no blue bicycle only her in this place that can't be described.

Tale of the Vast White

IN THE LANE BESIDE YOUR PARENT'S HOUSE IN KHON KAEN A WEED grows in the cement wall. It never flowers but is always green. A stubborn reminder that the earth is ever at the ready. You tell me that the soul is vast. *Like space* I ask. *Different* you say. Intricate and pliable like space but it is not an amalgam of matter and antimatter. It is not space surrounded by space, or the piercing of light. It is a distance travelled. A place to huddle in, to pause, to calibrate. Calculate. But it shrinks the moment you think of it and expands again later. A single soul is the size of the universe. *Vast like* that you say.

Tale of the Letter

IT ARRIVES IN TODAY'S MAIL. JOHN RECOGNIZES THE HANDWRITING and the return address of course and so even more reason not to open it. He sets it to one side. He can guess what it says and even begins to formulate a reply but then Nancy drives into the yard and parks beside his Volkswagen and he leaves his office and goes out to greet her. She's brought Tim, her son, with her and her dog Oscar. Tim is five and loves Oscar, and John knows that his grandson won't go anywhere in the car without Oscar.

He's just a dog, he told her. When Nancy was young, she'd been attached to her cat Muffin and wanted to take her everywhere and it was a half a year before she got used to leaving Muffin at home. Sometimes she would ask from the back of the car if Muffin was okay and they would always say that she was just fine and that cats didn't really like cars as all the movement scared them. *Really,* Nancy would say every time and they would say *Really* back.

Tim is wearing a red t-shirt and blue shorts as it is July and very hot. He helps Oscar get out of the car as Oscar is quite old and has arthritis in his hips and back legs. He's a brown Cocker Spaniard and likely was a frisky dog when he was younger but he's slow now and even a bit lethargic. Nancy has said he's a perfect dog for Tim because Oscar is a calming influence on him. Nancy had always been such an agreeable and easy child that John wonders how Tim could be the exact opposite. They've had to put him in a special kindergarten class because he wouldn't sit still in a regular class.

I was hoping you'd watch Tim for a bit. I should have called but I thought it would be okay. I have a procedure in town it will take about an hour.

He says that is fine. He knows well enough what she means by a procedure do doesn't ask and she doesn't say anything more about it.

Good I've brought him some lunch and a bag of treats that he only gets if he eats his lunch and is well behaved. You have to hold him to that.

I will, he says but knows he likely won't. He has a soft spot for the boy. Maybe because he'd always wanted a son or because of what life had been like when he was a boy.

Nancy hugs him and gets back into her Honda and is gone back down his short road to the main highway. Tim takes his hand and says, *Can Oscar and I go inside Grandpa?*

Sure.

He might need to pee. He peed and pooped earlier but he often pees in the afternoon too or when he gets excited. If he barks a lot that means he has to pee.

John is very familiar with the process by now but lets his grandson explain it.

Would you like some lunch?

Maybe in a little while. I had some potato chips before we came here. Did my mom pack some pop?

He checks the bag and sees a UVH container of apple juice. *Apple Juice.*

I hate Apple Juice. It's too sweet. You can give me some water instead. Oscar likes water. He doesn't like apple juice though. I gave him some once and he took a couple of licks and walked away.

John opens the front door and they all go inside. Oscar stays by the door even though he's been in this house dozens of times. Nancy got him from the animal rescue place in Nanaimo where she gets all her pets. She says she feels it's the right thing to do. She's suggested to him several times that he get a dog but he's refused.

Tim walks around the living room and touches a couple of items as though this is the first time he's been here.

Grandma's dead right? He says. This is the first time he's said anything like this.

Yes, John says. Although the statement has taken him aback, he sees no point in avoiding it.

I miss her. She used to give me candy and tell me good stories. Do you miss her?

All the time. He supposes that Nancy has finally told Tim the truth as he's been asking for months now where Ruth is.

I think I'm hungry now, Tim says.

You just said a minute ago you were full.

I was full then. I'm not full now. Can I see her bedroom?

It's the same one you've been in hundreds of times.

But it's different now right?

Not really.

It must be different if she's dead. My mom says that grandma died of cancer, that they tried to fix her but couldn't. She says that happens a lot and that cancer is very bad.

He wishes that Nancy had let him know that she'd had this conversation already with Tim but then he is her son and that is her business. They haven't talked that much since Ruth died and he's blamed that on himself. He hasn't really felt like talking about any of it with anyone especially not Nancy. There are lots of things that he and Ruth talked about that she wanted him to share with Nancy and he will, just not yet.

He leads Tim to the door of the bedroom. He keeps it closed all the time now although Ruth and he rarely closed it after Nancy moved out. Oscar has stayed by the door and John has a suspicion that when Tim and he return from here there will be a fresh puddle of pee on the hardwood floor just by the front door. But that's for later.

He opens the door slowly and it creaks on the hinges. He doesn't remember it doing that before but maybe it has, and he just hasn't noticed it. Once the door is open all the way Tim goes straight to the bed and to the side that Ruth slept on. He leans forward there until his nose touches the covers. He's washed the bedding enough times by now that all he'll smell is the fragrance of the laundry soap but maybe to Tim that will still be his grandmother's smell.

John waits at the door and Tim straightens and goes to the window and looks out at the back garden. It's mostly green out there with a few late summer flowers.

She must miss this room, Tim says.

Yes. Would you like have some lunch now?

Okay, Tim says and takes John's head and walks towards the island in the middle of the open kitchen. John sees that there is a puddle of pee beside Oscar.

Sit here, he says and hoists Tim onto one of the wooden stools that circles the granite island. He then gathers a fist full of paper towels from the roll on the counter and goes to the door and soaks up the pee with them.

Uh Oh. I knew that would happen. Bad boy Oscar, Tim yells. *That's what mom says whenever Oscar does something bad. She says dogs are smart like people, but if they are too old, they can't be toilet trained.*

John washes his hands thoroughly in the kitchen sink and then takes out the lunch that Nancy prepared. Oscar has left the door now and sits at the base of Tim's stool. He rests his head on his front paws and John suspects that he will soon be asleep.

Yummy. Look what your mother made for you. John cuts the hot dog into small bite sizes portions like he did with Nancy when she was even younger than Tim is now.

You want Ketchup with that?

Yeah, I love Ketchup. Mom and Dad don't let me have it too often.

John retrieves the bottle from the fridge and has to wait for it to pour out.

Mom and Dad don't keep the Ketchup in the fridge. It pours faster then.

That was Ruth's doing. She kept many things in the fridge that didn't need to be in the fridge. She liked to be on the safe side she would say.

Tim eats his hot dog and the mashed potatoes and chopped carrots quickly. He leaves one piece of hot dog and two carrots for Oscar who eats those quickly.

Oscar would like some water, he says then and John takes down a plastic bowl from the cupboard and fills it with water and sets it down for Oscar. The dog drinks it all down right away, so John fills another bowl and Oscar sniffs at that and has several licks and then goes back to the front door and curls up there.

Grandpa can I play on your computer now?

Okay. Tim is already hooked on computer games and Nancy has said she and Phil have had to curtail his game playing otherwise he'd do it all the time.

He takes Tim into his office and lets him sit at his laptop. He opens a game for Tim and within seconds the boy is fully engrossed in it.

He, too, sits at his desk and takes the letter and holds it. He looks over at Tim who seems to have forgotten already that his grandfather is there.

The letter is from his brother Paul in Winnipeg, and he knows Paul will ask how he is doing. This will mean how is he doing since Ruth's death. He doesn't know how many times he has to tell Paul that he is fine before he leaves him alone. Before Ruth got sick Paul and he talked a few times a year on the phone. They never exchanged letters. After Ruth died Paul phoned more often. And John let it go to voice mail sometimes. That's when the letters started. Paul has started writing every week now. Mostly he doesn't say much that's new in the letter, so John doesn't really see the point of them. He answers when he's in the mood to answer. He reads each of Paul's letters only once and then adds it to the stack which is already substantial. He wonders when Paul will get tired of writing them. Although Paul is his older brother, at times he looks younger, and his wife Catherine is healthy as can be. He mentions her in the letters but never talks about how healthy she is. He is more sensitive in his letters than he remembers his brother being when they were growing up or how he is on the phone.

When they used to talk on the phone they'd always come around to politics and Paul has always been conservative while John always leans left. They had gotten in a few heated conversations over the phone with one of them hanging up on the other.

Now he wonders why they bothered to get so worked up. Thankfully Paul never mentions politics in his letters nor does John when he writes back. He always makes a point of asking about Catherine and their sons. Paul always asks about Nancy and Tim but rarely mentions Phil, and John wonders if he even remembers his name.

He runs his thumb under the sealed flap and is about to open the letter when Tim says, *Grandpa I'm stuck. Can you help?*

Sure, he says and sets the letter down and asks what he's stuck at. He's never played this game and only has it on his computer at Ruth's urging so there would be things for Tim to do.

There, Tim says and points a finger at the screen. John sees a soldier halfway up a ladder.

He supposed to fly from here, Tim says.

Have you tried going down the ladder and trying again? No.

Try that.

Okay.

He does and this time the soldier does fly a very long way and then lands in front of a castle.

Thank you, Grandpa. You're so smart.

John knows that he's just lucky that he's been around computers long enough to know that sometimes the best course of action is to backtrack. He wishes that worked in real life too. If it did, the first thing he would do is cancel Ruth's cancer. The second thing he would do is answer all of Paul's calls. Maybe the letters wouldn't have started, and they wouldn't be haunting him as much as they do.

Nancy comes back then and honks once. That means she's in a hurry and won't come in. He marshals Tim away from the laptop and back out to the front door. There's another puddle of pee but this one is smaller.

Bad dog Oscar. Bad dog. Tim says.

I'll take care of that don't worry. Let's get you out to the car. Your mommy is waiting.

He opens the door and waves to Nancy who waves back. Tim takes his hand and they walk to the car. Oscar follows very slowly behind them. Tim opens the back door on the passenger side and helps push Oscar into the back. Oscar curls up on the floor in front of the seat. John then opens the front door for Tim to get inside.

Tim climbs into his seat and John fastens the lap belt around him.

How was he? Nancy asks.

Terrific, Johns says, and tussles Tim's hair and Tim smiles up at him.

Good, Nancy says. *I'll call soon. Okay.*

He closes the door and watches through the car window as she slowly shifts into drive. She takes her foot off the brake pedal and the car inches forward in the gravel of his driveway. He stands where he is until the car turns at the highway and is gone.

Tale of Amber Eyes

THE CHRISTMAS MY FATHER DISAPPEARED STARTED AS FESTIVE AS ALL the others. I'd turned twelve that year and still thought of Christmas as the best time of the year, but that was about to change. On Christmas morning my younger brother, sister and I opened our few presents eagerly even though already knew what they were because we'd bought them for ourselves.

At some point, my father went to the wood stove and lifted the lid to put in more firewood. His eyes glowed amber in the firelight and I didn't stare at them long but turned back to my play. That year my brother and I got flashlights and monster puzzles. His was Frankenstein and mine was Dracula. I remember mine being mostly red and his mostly blue. My brother and I had our half- completed puzzles laid out side by side on the floor while my sister played with some windup toy. I think it was a deer or rabbit, but I don't remember exactly. My father returned to his armchair and took a long sip of his beer and then focused on the TV that he always had on even though we only got one channel, CBC Winnipeg. That meant that current events were easier to grasp then, not all the interference of opposing sides we have now.

My mother sat on the couch across from my father watching the TV too. I don't remember any of us talking much that day although my brother and mother and sister were usually very talkative unlike my father and me. My mother got up after a while and went and sat on the bed in their room. When I looked in on her later, she was crying. I asked her what was wrong, and she waved a hand as if to say that she had it under control. I know now that she didn't, but I believed her then. I returned to my puzzle and the few remaining unused pieces formed a small red pile to my right, facing my father.

By then, he was so engrossed in whatever was on TV that he looked like a robot turned off except that his eyes occasionally blinked and drifted from side to side as though tracking something. I returned to my puzzle and closed my eyes and attempted to put the remaining pieces in place using only my fingers to guide me. I thought I got most of them right but when I opened my eyes every single piece I'd added was in the wrong place. I ran a hand over the surface of the puzzle and felt those protruding pieces.

I took the puzzle apart and started over. When I glanced over at my brother, he'd done the same. That seemed to be the point of those puzzles. They were so easy to put together that we did that over and over just to feel each piece going into its rightful place. When the monsters were fully assembled, they weren't scary especially reduced to two dimensions. They looked as though they were lying on the floor. When I finished mine a second time, I stood and put a foot on top of Dracula just to see him disappear from view.

My father got up then and as he walked past me I heard a hissing sound as though air were leaking from him. I wanted to reach up and touch him as he passed but instead watched him move at a slow purposeful pace. When he got to the stove, I took my puzzle apart and closed my eyes and listened to the metal noises he made as he lifted the lid and set it to one side. Then I heard the hollow clunk of dry poplar being forced into the stove. He kept the lid off the opening until the wood fully caught fire and crackled. There was a minute more of cracks and pops (what was he doing?) before he scraped the cast iron lid along the stovetop and let it clang into place over that fiery opening. He didn't seem to be concerned about how noisy he was.

I reached then for the first puzzle piece I could grab without paying attention to where it might go. I set it down in front of me and selected another and another working my way out from the middle toward the edges.

My father didn't return to his chair but went outside, where it was cold and snowy, and stayed out there. I went to the door and opened it and saw that he was sitting in his truck with the engine running. I stood with the door open despite all the cold air rushing in. My brother and sister stopped what they were doing and looked in my direction but didn't say anything. The cold settled into my bones and my fingers stung but I still held the door open.

Eventually my father backed the truck up and then headed down the road. His taillights vanished almost immediately in the wildly blowing snow. I knew he was going to town to drink more beer and wouldn't be back until very late. It was Christmas Day but he knew places in town where he could still buy beer and sit and drink.

I shut the door and returned to my puzzle. My mother came out of their bedroom and went to the TV and turned up the volume and sat in his chair. My brother got up and went outside to pee. He was gone so long I almost got up to check on him, but he came back inside before I got the full urge. When he came in, he was covered in a light dusting of snow. He didn't have a coat on so was shaking noticeably. He went to the wood stove and put in more wood just as my father had done but he closed the lid right away and stayed there to warm up. He was nearly two years younger than me but even then had a better grasp than I of what was really going on.

My mother remained fixed on the TV show she was watching, and I gave up my puzzle and sat in the couch to watch with her. I am not sure what show was except that it was likely something Christmassy. Whatever it was would have depicted a very different Christmas from ours and took place far away maybe somewhere it didn't even snow. In it everyone would have been nice to each other and by the end everything got forgiven. I knew even then that those were the rules for Christmas. I also I realized then that my mother wouldn't ever forgive my father.

The four of us continued with our Christmas celebrations without my father as best we could. We had ample wood to keep the house warm. I pretended that I didn't miss him but in truth I wanted him there. I needed our family to be whole for one day a year, even if it meant he'd be held here against his will. I am no longer certain of the nobility of such a wish but then my father not being there had seemed a crime of significant proportions.

At some point I went out into the snow to pee too and aimed the beam of my new flashlight into the tire tracks of my father's truck. They were already partly filled in with fresh snow, but I could still see how he'd backed up at a sharp angle and then driven straight off. The tracks going away were steady despite the number of beers he'd already drank. I tried to imagine then what his thoughts were as he drove away. But I had no idea of them nor do I now beyond the urge to be somewhere else, somewhere he could let out what he'd been holding in.

Standing in that cold and shivering I didn't know then the dent that icy Christmas Day would put in all our lives. Then I imagined my father stumbling in later perhaps even tripping on some toy my sister or brother or I had left out. The house would be dark by then and chilly even as the fire would have burned down to embers. All of us four huddled under covers sleeping in whatever warmth we could find.

Only now from the distant lens of the future can I face the truth that the four of us woke the next day to a cold house. My brother or mother dressed first and started the fire. None of us went to a window to check to see if my father's truck was there because it wasn't. Nor did he return later that day or ever. He was simply gone for good. Only now can I admit how as soon as we rose that morning Christmas was over for good and any promise such a day had afforded it never would again. Christmas was the day my father disappeared. His truck was found buried in a snowbank next to a rock cut he'd managed to swerve and miss. But he wasn't in the truck nor were there discernable tracks leading from it because by then it had snow so much and so many vehicles had passed over that spot it was as though he'd never gotten out of the truck and yet he wasn't in it either.

His truck was hauled out by a tow truck and didn't have a scratch on and the engine ran perfectly fine. My mother would drive it for years after and then later my brother and I until it finally cratered more than decade later. By then my mother had become permanently committed to the mental hospital in Fort William and the three of us were old enough to make do on our own.

His body never turned up and all we know for certain is that he'd been on his way home. Likely too drunk to properly make out the highway and had simply skidded off when the truck hit black ice. It went into a snowbank only four miles from home. Perhaps in his drunken state he mistook the nearby power clearing for the highway and set off that way. Police believe he perished somewhere in all that deep snow and later in spring some wild animal dragged him too far off to be found.

While I was still in school, twice a day the school bus passed that spot where his truck went off the highway and I would often wonder if he was still out there somewhere having survived despite the odds. But I knew even then that that was a hopeful dream the living cling to when all logic suggests otherwise.

"Stop looking," my brother said to me many times when our mother was gone too and there was only the three of us. Still, I think often of that Christmas because it was my last Christmas until I had a family of my own and was able to start over again.

I have often wondered the exact moment that day when it all took a turn for the worse. I can't help thinking it was the moment when my father went to the stove to stuff in more wood. What he'd seen in the flames must have told him what he should do next.

I have often imagined that in those vital moments after his truck slide of the highway and he got out alive he'd thought he'd be fine. Everywhere he turned it would have been so thoroughly white. The snow would have picked up even more by then and been falling in such heavy flakes that I imagine him reaching out a hand like he must have done as a boy to catch a few of them just to feel them melt on his palm.

Nothing the least bit dangerous about snowflakes all on their own like that and yet in a few minutes or an hour at most it would be all over. There wouldn't have been any traffic on the highway at that hour especially in the middle of a snowstorm and he would have been susceptible to drunken logic and likely burrowed in somewhere and thought that would stay him warm there until morning. I doubt he even had time to sober up. That would have happened later when he was already dead, his body as stiff as the trees all around him heavy with snow.

But that isn't what happened and is only the depiction of the raw reversal of thought. My father did go to the fire and he did go outside but only to pee. In a few minutes he came back in the hose and returned to the chair and continued to watch the same TV show he'd been watching. My mother came out of the bedroom and sat on the couch across from him but leaned toward my father and he reached out a hand and she took it and they sat like that for the longest time.

I had completed my puzzle a second time by then and looked at it for a moment and specifically at the mouth of Dracula. I wanted him to be smiling but he wasn't. I then broke the puzzle apart piece by piece starting at the top right corner and worked my way toward the middle and from there down to the bottom left corner. When I had all of the pieces broken apart, I set them in the box the puzzle had come in and walked the box to the wood stove. I stopped there for a moment and through the open kitchen door I had a full view of the rest of my family. All of them had stopped what they were doing and were watching the Christmas show on TV. My brother had completed his puzzle too and it was on the floor beside him.

I opened the lid of the wood stove and watched flames move wildly about the pieces of wood my father had set there earlier. They were all fully engulfed and halfway burned through. I felt immediately the heat of those flames as the fire burned so hot I couldn't stand to leave the lid open for long. I lifted the puzzle box and tried to fit it through the round opening, but the rectangular box didn't fit. I slipped the lid handle out of its notch in the lid and used it to poke the box until it fell into the flames below. It didn't take long for it to ignite, and I watched the flames swirl around the box at first and then melt away to those jagged edged red pieces.

When a few of those caught fire, I set the lid back over the fire and knew that soon the puzzle box would be reduced to ash. I glanced toward the TV. Only my brother turned to look in my direction but not for long as he soon turned back to the TV too.

I stood for a moment longer at the stove as my father had done earlier and then returned to where I had been sitting before, but this time I focused on what was on TV. I watched that black and white drama and its grey world but felt incredibly happy.

Tale of the Mannequin

DELORES STOOD ON THE SIDEWALK BUT VERY NEAR TO THE SHOP window. She watched the woman on the other side of the glass dress a female mannequin. The mannequin was smiling but had no hair nor makeup and was naked from the waist up. The woman dressing her had put on a pleated flannel skirt with a checkered pattern. A very trendy look for 1915. The mannequin also wore black flats much the same as Delores wore. She looked down at her own and saw how scuffed hers were. She scraped dust and dirt off one using the other. This put her a bit off balance, and she rested a hand on the shop window for support.

The sound of that must have alerted the woman dressing the mannequin because she turned around and nodded at Delores but didn't smile. She didn't look annoyed either, or surprised. She must have been used to people watching her by now Delores decided.

She took her hand off the glass and the woman turned back to her work. This part of Portage Avenue in Winnipeg wasn't that busy this early in the morning. Delores had an hour before she had to be at the phone exchange where she worked as an operator. She spent her days plugging and unplugging phones lines. She was so used to the tiny voices in her head that she often heard them when she was away from work like now.

He's such a strange friend a woman had said to another woman yesterday. Delores knew their names and that they called each other every day but she refused to remember their names away from work. They were just caller one and caller two to her.

How is he strange? The other woman had asked. Her voice was much higher pitched and more nasal than her friend's, whose voice was lower and gruff sounding, almost masculine except when she talked fast. Then her voice was higher but not as high as her friend's. Yesterday she'd talked very fast.

You know. Like that, she said.

Really like that? Her friend had said.

Delores knew it was a code how they talked on the phone knowing the operator could hear everything they said if she so chose, and she did. She knew that they were talking about sex and that the friend the first woman was talking about wasn't just a friend but a lover. A boyfriend maybe although she never said his name on the phone and so it was known to each of them and not necessary.

Delores can't remember his name ever coming up except as *he* and *friend.*

He has to work early. Just left. At the door. You know?

Her friend didn't answer but waited perhaps expecting more and soon enough there was.

He brought a book and chocolates. It was a book I'd already read months ago and raved to him about so not sure why he gave it to me except to say he'd been listening and not listening.

What book is that? the other woman asked.

The first woman said the name, but Delores didn't recognize it. She read a lot, but it wasn't a book she'd heard of or read.

What are you going to do with it? You can have it if you want it.

Okay.

I'll call you tomorrow, the first woman had then said.

Okay, the second woman said. That was all code too and it likely meant that they worked together and that they saw each other at work and talked and gossiped. Or so Delores imagined. The second woman rarely divulged any details from her life. Mostly she listened and responded to the first woman. Delores imagined the first woman living in a house and the second in an apartment based on what they've said and the parts of the city their numbers indicated that they live.

The dresser had now put a white blouse on the mannequin. The blouse had a puffy collar and cuffs. This was not a blouse that Delores would ever wear. She knew that the woman dressing the mannequin would put a jacket on next and that it would gather at the hips and match the checkered pattern in the skirt. The mannequin would not be dressed for work like Delores was dressed now but for leisure like going out to the theatre or cafés along Main Street. That was not a part of the city Delores went to often because she couldn't afford the theatre on her salary. Instead, she went to the library at least once a week and signed out novels and read those in the evenings. Most of the novels took place in England or America and none in Winnipeg. She had never read a novel that took place in Winnipeg and couldn't imagine what such novel would be about except love maybe. Perhaps it would be about the lives of those two women on the phone yesterday or this woman dressing the mannequin or even the mannequin, but it wouldn't be about Delores. She was certain of that.

She was right about the jacket and the sleeves on it were short enough that the puffy cuffs of the blouse poked out the ends. She liked that look and wouldn't have thought of it herself, so she was glad she's stayed to see that part. She waited now to see what wig the woman put on the mannequin. It would either be blonde or brunette that wouldn't be confused with black hair or red hair like her own. The woman would then put a hat on top of the wig and Delores considered the two possibilities: a large flaring hat or a small demure, almost invisible hat made from straw or wool and not felt or fur. It was late spring so too warm for a fur hat.

Delores bet the wig would be blonde and it was. The cut of the hair was short and well above the shoulders like her own. The hair style of a woman who worked but this mannequin wasn't dressed for work. The hat the woman chose was a small straw hat that had a white band and the colour of the straw matched the blonde wig.

Now that the mannequin was fully dressed, she resembled many of the women that Delores passed in the street. These women didn't dress like the women at work. She imagined that the first woman on the phone yesterday looked like the mannequin. She imagined her stopping at this window often to get ideas for how to dress and then going inside and making a purchase.

She imagined her ordering whatever she wanted and didn't worry about the cost.

Delores turned in the direction of work just as the woman dressing the mannequin was tying a silk scarf around the neck of the mannequin. Delores imagined the woman finishing her job and then turning around already knowing that Delores would no longer be there.

At the next corner a man a little older than her and dressed for work crossed from the other side of the street and he raised his felt hat to her and nodded and then continued on his way. She didn't look back to watch him go but crossed the street and passed more familiar shops with window displays but she didn't stop to take in any of those displays but continued at a faster pace now being only a block from work.

She knew that at exactly 4:00 PM the first woman would call the second woman. That was the pattern she was used to. There would be no follow up from yesterday's conversation. Nor would the book ever be mentioned again, but somewhere during their course of conversation the first woman would declare again, what a strange friend the man was, and the second woman would ask how he was strange. This time as Delores listened, she would think of that mannequin and the woman dressing her and how still the mannequin had been and how even fully dressed she wouldn't be going anywhere.

Tale of When It Rained for Two Million Years

BECAUSE OF *THE WET INTERMEZZO* PERIOD THERE IS LOVE, CONIFER forests, and, for a time, dinosaurs. It rained for two million years and then the Earth dried. He thinks about this now as he often does each morning as he waits for the bus. He rides it to the same coffee shop and orders the same breakfast and the darkest and strongest coffee they have. He doesn't add cream or sugar.

When Donna was still alive, she would put cream and sugar in her coffee, and he would do the same. They would sip their coffees together on the back deck in the warmer months. In winter, they would sit at the kitchen table they'd bought at Ikea when the kids were still young. Donna did most of the talking and he'd contribute now and then usually when she'd ask him a question. She was keen on politics and had worked as a geologist for Esso. She rarely talked about geology though except to tell him about the time it rained for two million years.

He had trouble conceptualizing that many years.

She'd told him that he wasn't alone in that, and that *deep time was difficult to grasp*. She'd say that *a million seconds is only 12 days but a billion seconds is 32 years and that 130 billion seconds was 4100 years. That's the scale of deep time.*

That also meant that their life together lasted a little over a billion seconds. The morning she died they hadn't talk about deep time. They were busy saying that they loved each other. He'd held her hand in the hospital and she'd opened her eyes one final time and smiled. He'll never forget that smile it meant to him that she was happy he was there.

Afterwards their two daughters cried for the rest of the day, and he didn't cry at all not until he was alone at the kitchen table where they'd had so many coffees. He looked across to her side and couldn't fully comprehend how she wasn't there anymore although the logic of it was perfectly clear. He conjured her there and listened to her tell him again about *the wet intermezzo*. He loved how she said those words with such urgency.

The bus arrives right on time, and he is slower to climb the steps now, but it is always the same driver, and she doesn't hurry him and instead smiles at him as he drops his coins in the box. She always nods at him before she loses the door but never drive away from the stop until Stan is sitting down. He and Donna never took this bus, he always drove them places, but he hasn't driven in a decade now. It's been a long decade without Donna. Still, she's with him every day.

The bus stops out front of the coffee shop he has been going for breakfast since Donna died. He's a regular there and knows all the server's names but they don't know his and he likes it that way.

Usually, he reads the paper as he waits for his breakfast and coffee. He prefers the sports section and the entertainment section and avoids the front page or anything to do with politics. He considers all that unseemly now.

He always has his eggs sunny side up and his toast dry, not buttered. He likes to put each egg on top of a slice of toast and poke the soft yoke and watch the yellow liquid flow out and over the toast. The eggs and toast taste perfect together and he never gets tired of them even yearns for that taste each morning when he wakes up. He likes to wash that down with dark, bitter coffee. The taste of coffee lingers until he has lunch later at home.

He once asked Donna how it is possible for it to rain for two million years. She said it wasn't continuous, but most days were rainy like winter days on the west coast of Canada. She told him that volcanos in Alaska and British Columbia triggered the rain

Volcanoes? He'd asked.

She explained how all that ash and smoke formed clouds and once the rain started it didn't stop until the planet became green and lush again. By then very different creatures roamed the Earth including dinosaurs.

They'd only been to Vancouver and Victoria once in the winter for a three-week holiday, and it rained most of the time. He hadn't minded the greyness of the sky because the lawns were green in January instead of covered in snow.

Today he sits at the counter to have his breakfast and when he is nearly done a man at least a decade younger than him sits beside him on his right. The man orders a breakfast when the server comes.

When Stan has finished his breakfast and is on his second cup of coffee the man asks him if this is his first time coming here. Stan says he has been coming here every day for nearly a decade. The man says he has too, but he's never seen Stan here before today. Stan says he's never seen him either.

The man pushes his half-finished plate to one side and Stan wonders if he does that every morning. Is it as much a part of his routine as Stan putting his eggs on his toast and puncturing the soft yokes? He doesn't ask the man about this but decides it is his routine and prefers to think of it that way. Stan also doesn't ask the man if he is married because he wouldn't be here if he was.

They don't say anything more for the longest time as Stan and the man sip their respective coffees. Stan gets a second refill while the man puts his hand over his cup when the server offers to top his up too. Stan expects him to say something about this when the server moves away but he doesn't. Instead, he takes a final sip of coffee and puts the cup down next to his plate, so both are now to his right and away from Stan.

This refill is cooler than the other one and Stan finishes the whole cup in several long sips.

"Alright," the man says then and taps the counter and gets up and says that it is nice to have met Stan. He doesn't ask Stan's name, nor does he offer his. He goes to the front counter and pays, and after he does, he looks in Stan's direction and waves.

Stan is certain that he will never see this man again. The server hasn't gathered up the man's dirty dishes and Stan looks at them again and notices that the man's eggs are sunny side up too but that he hasn't put the eggs on top of his toast but keeps them separate. The toast is moist from butter, and he has spread some raspberry jam but only in the very middle of each slice of toast and has eaten toward that from the round top part of the toast leaving the squared bottom corners untouched.

When he looks in the direction of the counter again, the man is gone. He doesn't know if the man walked here or drove or took the bus, but it doesn't make a difference. No matter how he came here Stan will never see him again. Most mornings when he comes here the other patrons and staff will be the same, but that man will never be amongst them. He will either have eaten earlier or will come after Stan leaves. He doesn't know what has changed the man's routine today and caused him to appear here at the same time as Stan but whatever that change is, it won't persist, and he'll go back to his regular routine.

Stan pays at the front counter and leaves a sizeable tip for the server as he does every morning. When he steps outside it is cloudy, but he knows it won't rain. He crosses the street to the other side to catch the same bus number home.

He'd asked Donna how scientist knew about this two-million-years of rain, and she'd told him, they'd studied rock deposits and that it took decades of study to come to this conclusion.

So, it isn't a hundred percent for certain? He'd asked.

No but pretty close to it, she'd said.

He'd liked it that she'd been honest about that as she was about everything else in her life. She was a truthful person for whom truth was vital. He is the same and senses that that man today is too. Stan believes that he has eaten in the same café as the man for the past ten years without them ever seeing each other. If they ever do meet again, Stan plans to tell him about *the wet intermezzo* because he senses that like most people, the man doesn't know about it or deep time.

Tale of the High Heart

THE BOY CAME TO THE POND AND STOOD AT THE EDGE. IT WAS THE hottest day of the summer, and he had the urge to strip and dive in. But instead, he watched a frog sitting on a lily pad. It was a large frog and a large lily pad. The sun was directly overhead and so hot that sweat beaded down his brow and he wiped that away several times with a forearm. *Listen* Kurt heard the frog say but of course the frog didn't speak and couldn't speak in any way that the boy could understand. The water around the lily pad was such a dark brown that if the boy dove in and swam beneath the surface and opened his eyes, he wouldn't be able to see more than a few inches in front of him. He'd have to surface and when he did the sky would be so bright and utterly blue that he couldn't look there without hurting his eyes.

You don't need to explain what you are thinking for all is known. Even you here at the edge of this pond across the highway from the lake you usually swim in where the water is clear you can see well in front of you under water.

That voice Kurt knew. It wasn't the frog's voice or either of boy's parents. It was a voice from a recurring dream. In it he stood in light rain and was waiting for someone. A stranger appeared as they often did in his dreams. This stranger offered him an umbrella and said similar words to those he'd heard just now and in a similar voice.

You must have a high heart and your kindness so broad that there is nothing else in any direction. Those eggs you had for breakfast the spinach you had for dinner yesterday those are necessary.

What is a high heart? Kurt asked now in his head.

Kindness. The voice answered.

That is all?

Yes, that is all. But do not swim here nor pay attention to the frog it is merely on the lily pad because it is a frog.

What did good was also good the boy knew, and he knelt and reached forward and placed the fingers of his right hand in that brown water of the pond. The water was warm to the touch, but his fingers were distorted by the brown water and no longer looked like his. That startled him and he pulled his hand out of the water. At that moment he heard the frog jump into the pond. The splash that made was nearly imperceptible, but he heard it and knew if he searched around he would spot the top of the frog's head just above the surface of the water

The sky was once where humans expected to flee to when they died and then later the earth and later still the sea. But when someone dies, they go to none of those places. They simply return to a different story than this one.

Am I a story? Kurt asked.

Yes.

A happy one?

Yes. All stories are happy. How is that possible?

It is just possible. There is no need to doubt it or go against that because to go against it is to resist and to resist is to not have a high heart. To be human is to be happy and to be happy is human.

That sounds the same and yet contradicts.

You are a smart boy Kurt, but don't depend too much on that. Instead depend on your urges. They are the most powerful and the purist guide to truth.

Kurt stopped listening then or perhaps the voice stopped speaking he wasn't exactly sure which it was. Instead, he stood and wiped his wet hand against the leg of his pants and then waved it in the air to let the sun dry the rest.

He searched around for the frog and didn't see it anywhere and thought that likely it was below the surface of the pond or hiding amongst the lily pads and bull rushes.

He took the same narrow path that he came here on. Along the way he looked to both sides of the path and noted the various ferns, tall grass, Saskatoon bushes, poplars, thick spruce, and balsam trees.

This was a garden, and he was in very center of it.

Ready your high heart he thought as he walked, and the more he walked the better sense he had of a high heart and exactly what it meant.

The *high heart is in everyone. The fruit in this garden. Ripe, ready. No dream. All a dream.*

Tale of the Paint Brush

THE ELEVATOR CHIMES AND THE ELEVATOR DOORS OPEN. A MAN AND woman step out of it. In his left arm, he holds a paper bag full of groceries. He walks slightly behind the woman, and she reaches the door of their apartment first. It is three doors down from the elevator and she takes a set of keys from her purse and unlocks the door and then puts the keys back in her purse and snaps it shut. She goes into the apartment first and the man steps in behind her. She takes off her long coat and hangs it on a hook near the front door and he walks the bag of groceries through the swinging kitchen door and lets it sway behind him. He sets the bag on the counter next to the sink and woman comes into the kitchen and stops the door from swaying before coming to the counter and standing next to the man.

Let me help, she says

Alright, he says. He talks out a cartoon of whole milk, two cans of sardines, a pound of butter and two large pork chops wrapped in brown paper. He hands each item to the woman, and she puts some in the fridge and others in the cupboard. He doesn't hand her the pork chops but holds them in one hand and turns the brown pager over to check for blood stains, but there are none.

She gets down a dinner plate from the stack in the cupboard and hands it to him. He sets the wrapped pork chops on the plate. He doesn't unwrap them but leaves them like that. She opens the fridge door, and he sets the plate on the top shelf of the fridge which is mostly empty except for the cartoon of milk

32

that she has put in the top right corner. He sets the plate in the very middle of the tray and below the milk. He looks at those two items and knows in a week both will be gone but for now they share the fridge.

Food is strange he thinks although he's not really sure why he thinks that. He checks the fridge door and sees where she has properly set the pound of butter. Later one of them will take it out and cut of a quarter pound slice and set that in a butter dish and put it in the cupboard so it is soft and easily spread. He'll fry the pork chops for dinner in some of that butter and she will boil carrots and chop cucumbers. *They eat healthily* he thinks. They have that in common and a love deeper than any he's felt before. They are matched although they don't talk about it that way. He thinks it and knows that she thinks it.

When they make love, sometimes he feels transported as though he's become separated from his body and in those moments no matter how wild and uncontrollable his thoughts are they always meld. He assumes it is the same for her although they have not discussed this.

He hears running in the hall then. Children running. He doesn't open the door as he knows it will be the same two boys that are often running in the hall. They live somewhere in the building although he is not certain where. They once rode the elevator with Sally and him, but the boys didn't speak. They were all fidgety energy the way boys often are and how he had been once but isn't now. His mother has told him recently that he rarely stood still for long as a boy, and she'd often complained to him then that he behaved as though he had ants in his pants. He has no recollection of such a conversation with her.

Sally has gone to the spare bedroom. The one that was going to the kid's room but that's impossible now. She will have taken out her easel and paint brush and will be making a new colour. He tries to conjure the colour in his head, but all he can imagine are colours she has already created. She always makes new colours whenever she paints. He will ask her the name of the colour she will say it doesn't have a name, that she's just created it.

He stops at the front door and hears another burst of footsteps. The younger boy is always chasing the older boy and soon the footsteps fade, and he knows they've gone into the stairwell. He hears Sally humming and that means that she is already painting. He goes to the door of that room and pauses before entering it and thinks of a deep orange so deep it is part red and part purple but still orange.

How can a colour like that have a name he wonders. He opens the door, and she is painting a sky and the colour is so real that it immediately recognizable as sky even though it isn't blue or grey but some shade in between that is a perfect sky colour. He instinctively looks out the window to compare it, but the sky today is a gun metal grey smear of storm clouds.

He backs out of the room not wishing to disturb her in this moment. Later she will show him what she has painted today and ask if he came into the room while she was painting as she will have the sensation he was there, but no direct memory of it. He goes to their bedroom and sits on the bed for a moment. He closes his eyes and finds every edge of himself internally, and only when he has gathered all of that into his continuing thoughts, does he get up and go to the closet and open that heavy wooden door there.

Sometimes it sticks where the bottom binds on the floor but not today. It swings freely and he stands holding the doorknob and leans on that for support. On the top shelf where previous tenants may have kept hats or shoe boxes of pictures there's an accordion. He takes it down and carries it back to the bed and sets it beside him when he sits down. He unsnaps the locking straps on the bottom and top and then puts his left hand in the leather handle.

He's adjusted that so he can slide his hand up and down in there and reach the bass keys if he were to press them. He rests his right hand under the corner of the main keyboard to support the accordion and then pulls it close to his chest. He holds the air release button in and opens and closes the accordion several times. It makes no sound except the sound of air going in and out. He rests his right hand below the keyboard to support it. He doesn't press any of the keys and truly has no idea which ones to press when anyway. Two more times he opens and closes the accordion and two more times he listens to air going in and out.

He's never really played it. It was his brother's and when he died it came to him. The most he's ever done with it is what he's done just now. *I hope you learn to play it,* his brother had said only months before he died. But John never has. He's never been that fond of accordion music. He prefers guitars and pianos and vocals. Instead, he imagines that his brother's final breaths are trapped inside the accordion and every time he hears that air going in and out, his brother is breathing again, wherever he is. He's been dead five years and John still hasn't learned to play the accordion. He hasn't signed up for lessons or even watched any instruction videos on YouTube.

He presses the accordion back together again and listens to that long last exhale. He takes his hands out of the left handle and sets the accordion beside him on the bed and snaps the locking straps back on. He carries the accordion to the closet and sets it on that high shelf again. He doesn't close the closet door but returns to the edge of the bed. He stays there a good while and eventually Sally comes in and sits beside him on the bed. She smells of paint and brush cleaner and even of paint brush although he can't really describe that smell only has a fleeting sensation of it.

I'm finished. Do you want to see what I've done? Yes.

They sit for a moment longer there on the bed. In time she puts her arm around his shoulder, and he puts his arm around her waist.

They don't speak. In time, they stand together and go out into the hall. He hears steps hurry past the front door but doesn't look in that direction. Instead, they go into her room and the first thing he sees is her painting facing him and every colour and shape in it is beyond anything he would have imagined. Her paint brush is sitting in a plastic margarine dish and the brushed tip up so it can dry. All the colours have been washed off it so that it is ready to apply whatever colour she mixes next.

Tale of the Dancing Owl

DAN BOUGHT THE DANCING OWL IN A TOY STORE MORE THAN A decade ago. It's a windup toy and after it is cranked the owl hobbles from side to side more like a penguin. He has it on his desk to the right of all his papers and notes. Whenever he feels stressed, he likes to wind up the owl and watch it dance. The owl doesn't hoot or make any owl sounds. Instead, there's only the whirl and grinding of gears from its inner workings. The owl starts out dancing very fast but slows down and eventually stops.

Every morning when he arrives at work, the first thing he does is pick up the owl and turn the crank on the top of its head until it is fully wound up and then sets it down to dance. He takes the owl's dancing as good omen for the rest of the day. He can't think of what possessed him to buy it and yet now he can't imagine his workday without it.

Sometimes later in the day, if he's feeling stressed, he'll pick up the owl and crank it again and watch it dance. If he is particularly stressed, he'll do this until he gets bored and lets the owl wind down. He leaves it where it stops and goes back to work.

When it sits motionless on his desk, it looks more like an owl because it has the beak, eyes, and talons of an owl. He has wondered who designed the owl and decided how it should dance. Every aspect of the owl's dance is wrong, but he derives pleasure from it all the same. *There is no explaining that.*

It is during one of the times he's watching the dancing owl that his phone rings and Liz is calling.

Hello she says.

And just like that his life changes. The dancing owl has stopped but he continues to look at it as he waits for Liz to go on.
Is it raining there? she asks.
No, he says and wonders why she would ask him that?
Good. I need you to come over. Now?
Yes, she says and hangs up.
Dan gets up from his desk, leaves his office, and takes the elevator to the car parkade. It is brightly lit and he has no trouble finding his car. Once inside it he just sits there. *He could stay right here.* He thinks and then as soon as he thinks that he starts the engine and backs out of the stall and drives to her apartment building and parks out front.

It hasn't rained the whole time he's been driving but it is raining now. Just a light rain but enough to cause him to hesitate a moment in the car. He watches a woman and her young daughter come out of the front door of the building. The woman opens an umbrella and holds it over her daughter rather than herself. They pass his car and continue in direction of the busier street to the south of here.

Once they have passed, he gets out of the car and his suit and hair get wet as he runs to the door of her building. He stands in the vestibule where the intercom system is but doesn't buzz her apartment although she will be waiting. He studies the number pad and knows the numbers he needs to enter but looking at the keypad and all the numbers and the many possible combinations, each one like a gateway to a different life than this one. He believes he knows why she's asked him here. But he could also be wrong.

He finally enters the numbers to call her apartment and hears it ring seven times and then it stops. He enters them again. The same seven rings and then it stops again. He does this a third time and the same seven rings. A young man enters the vestibule then and walks past him and opens the front door with a key. He follows after him, and the man doesn't ask him where he was going or accost him in any way but goes to the waiting elevator and gets inside.

He takes the stairs instead not wishing to engage in conversation with the young man or explain where he's going. He runs up the five flights and is wheezing by the time he reaches there. He stops in the hallway to catch his breath. He doesn't want her to see him like this.

He then walks the full length of the hallway to her apartment and knocks on the door. When she doesn't answer he rings the doorbell twice. Still no answer. He tries the doorknob but it's locked. He takes out the key she's given him, and he opens the door and enters quietly not sure what to expect.

Hello, Dan says at the door but gets no reply. He says it twice more as he passes the kitchen and goes down the hallway to the bedroom. That door is open. He glances inside and sees that the bed is made.

Hello, he says again. Nothing. He goes back down the hall to the kitchen and says *Hello* again, and again nothing.

He opens the door to the fridge not sure even why except that being in the kitchen seems to warrant it. The fridge is crammed full of food, and he wonders how she could find anything in it. He takes out a jug of milk and sets it on the marble counter and then opens a black laminated cupboard door where he knows the glasses are and takes down a tall glass and fills it half full with milk. He takes one sip of the milk and coughs. It's sour. He pours the rest of the contents of the glass down the sink and then does the same with the jug and then runs cold water down the drain to make sure the sour milk is fully washed down. He drops the jug into the garbage under the sink. The garbage is nearly full and needs emptying, but he manages to push the jug down enough into it that it fits. He then rinses the glass and sets it in the dish tray to dry.

He goes back down the hall toward the bedroom but stops at the bathroom. That door is open too and he goes inside and sees that the bathtub is three quarters full of water, He tests the temperature of water with a finger and it's lukewarm. He rolls up his shirt sleep and reaches far down in the water and releases the rubber plug and the water begins to drain. He dries his hand and arm on a green towel hanging on the rack and then folds it and sets it back. He leaves the bedroom and goes back to the bedroom and directly to the bed. He lies down on it with all his clothes on.

Dan curls up into a fetal position and stays like that and then screams as at the top of his lungs. He screams and screams as loud as he must have when he was a baby and needed something. He screams until he had nothing left in him to scream out. He keeps his eyes closed and sees in his head the dancing owl on his desk and realizes then how silly and out of place it looks there and wonders again how he could have bought such a silly thing and why once he did, it brought him such pleasure and happiness. He wonders *what exactly the mechanism of that is.*

He tries to recall the shop where he bought it but can only recall that it had been a toy shop. He doesn't remember the salesperson who rang up his purchase or where even what street the store is on. He doesn't recall a single thing about the purchase including how much he'd paid for it. Only that now he has it and that it's still there on his desk where he left it. He screams again longer and louder, and when he's finished, he knows that will do the trick.

Dan waits then and listens and soon enough he hears Liz open the front door of the apartment and come down the hall. He gets up then off the bed and goes out in the hall to meet her. She's out of breath. She's been running.

Tale of the Missing Vowels

LATELY SHE'D BEGUN TO DROP THE LAST VOWEL IN CERTAIN WORDS. She wasn't exactly sure when this habit developed but her supervisor at work pointed it out recently and ever since she'd noticed whenever she did it. Janice could even feel when it was about to happen but wasn't able to stop it. Most people didn't seem to notice and only her supervisor Marsha had even mentioned it. At first, she suspected it was due to a misaligned bite because for weeks she'd been feeling significant pain in her right jaw. But when she went to the dentist and had her bite tested the dentist said her bite was perfectly aligned. Not a single tooth biting wrong. She asked him to test again and got the same results, so she asked again and got the same results.

She wasn't home long from the dentist when she felt the pain return to her right jaw and felt the tendons tighten as she chewed her food. She knew that had to be the culprit that made it harder for her to say certain sounds. The 'b' sound in particular and certain vowels that required more tense muscles like 'ee' and 'eh'.

Before all this, she'd spoken freely at work and had never given much thought to 'how' words were formed in her mouth but only on the meaning of what she was saying. Now she focused more on the mechanics of each word, and she felt somewhat untethered from meaning. Others at work would sometimes look at her oddly after she'd said something in a meeting. She'd replay her words in her mind and not hear the problem but clearly it had not sounded like she had anticipated.

In time she couldn't say certain words correctly anymore and she refrained from using those words to avoid confusion. *See and set* she could no longer say at all, and it occurred to her then that her mind had misplaced some vowels and she could still hear them in her mind when she was about to say them but those were not the ones she said.

She went to a voice coach and the coach had her doing voice practices in front of a mirror. She would say *ee* over and over and even certain *oo and it* sounds. She asked the coach if anything like this had happened to anyone else and the coach said often enough. She asked what would have caused that. The coach said that sometimes a mild stroke and other times just stress. It most often happened when someone had trouble relaxing.

She was only thirty-two, so she knew she was too young to have had a stroke. Besides she's not even been married although she had been in love five times. Her most recent relationship ended seven months ago. Ryan that time. Four times she'd love men and once a woman. Clarissa who always said that her name was a great grandmother's name.

Janice had never said anything derogatory about her name and had in fact liked it and liked to say it when they were making love. But that only lasted for a year because Clarissa smelled bad or to be precise had an off-putting body odour, and no matter how many times she showered using scented soaps, the odour always returned every time they made love. She didn't have a clue where Clarissa was now except far east somewhere like Toronto or Montreal. A city for certain because she was a city person.

Janice knew exactly where all the men she'd loved were now. Ryan lived in an apartment building in Calgary and four blocks east of hers. He was a geophysicist and worked in oil and gas. They hadn't communicated since the breakup. She hadn't love him but he instigated the breakup. She didn't love anymore any of the people she'd once been powerfully in love with. She hadn't known that was possible until it happened. When she was a teenager, she thought love was more permanent than that. She assumed that once she fell in love with someone that she would be in love with them for the rest of her life. She had been surprised to learn that love could fade and not last.

She was happy that she no longer loved any of those she once loved and was no longer troubled by any of that lost love. She liked that that gave her the freedom to fall in love again. Of course, that was all complicated now by the *vowel thing*. That was what she called it.

Her voice coach had warned her that such afflictions tended to get worse. She asked if that meant she'd lose the ability to speak because the thought of that terrified her.

Not at all. You'll just sound different than you used to. It happens more often than you may think. Most people talk the way they always talk until they get older and then their speech slows down, and falters. They eventually slur words and by the end mostly mumble.

But Janice wasn't faltering. She was just misplacing certain vowels, shifting some. Some she dropped and others she said differently than she used to with a peculiar accent unlike any she'd heard. Most people in Calgary didn't speak with accents or not at least any that she noticed. They talked like the people on TV and in the movies from America. She didn't have a name for that accent except common English. But those in movies and TV shows from the UK, Ireland, India, Caribbean, Australia, and New Zealand did speak English with noticeable accents and had peculiar sayings like: *Good on you* from Australia or *Oi* and *So it is* in Ireland.

When she stood in front of the bathroom mirror and practiced, she watched the shapes her mouth made as she said various sounds.

She hadn't ever paid attention to that before and simply said whatever word she wanted without giving the word a moment's thought.

Her voice coach showed her the different way she used her tongue to say certain sounds. That meant that the tip, front, centre and back of the tongue produced different sounds, and her coach got her to focus on the placement of her tongue as she practiced. Even in front of the mirror she soon lost track of what she was supposed to be watching for. Mostly her mouth just moved, and the words came out. She couldn't track were in her mouth her tongue was for any given sound except for certain obvious and very low sounds like *sat*.

Ryan was a smoker and smoked everywhere including in his car and in his apartment. He'd ask her, *Do you mind?* and then light up right away. It took her a while to realize he wasn't really asking but rather simply warning here that he was about to light a cigarette. She knew the smoking would kill him one day and she'd subtly hinted at that expecting him to catch on and quit. But he always rationalized his smoking. Although he could be reasonable about any other topic, on smoking, he would state the most obvious rationalization but not see them as rationalization. Whenever she would challenge him on them, he would act as though what he said made perfect sense. At first, she thought he was putting her on, but she soon realized that he truly believed what he said and that he would be the one exception who wouldn't be killed by smoking and that he'd be just fine. He even claimed that he didn't inhale but she'd watched him smoking enough to know he actually inhaled quite deeply.

She had worried that inhaling all that secondhand smoke had damaged her larynx and she'd asked her vocal coach about that, and she reassured Janice that it would take many decades for that kind of effect to show up, if ever. She'd been reassured by that, but also wished to blame someone especially Ryan as he was someone worthy of blame.

Recently Marsha called her into her office, and she hummed and hawed at first after asking Janice to sit in the seat in front of her desk. This was the first time that Janice has been in Marsha's office since Marsha had become her supervisor and she felt her stomach knot from worry.

Are you having trouble with alcohol or some other substance? Marsha finally asked her.

God no, she'd said and that was absolutely true. Then after a second, she thought to ask, *Why?*

You've been slurring your words lately. Slurring my words?

Yes, slurring your words. I'm not the only one whose noticed. Several people have brought it to my attention.

I don't slur my words, Janice said.

Yes, you do. And often of late. Often now in meetings I can't understand much of what you say. Others are watching. I don't know what to do. You do your job well but slurring your words on the job. Well, you know?

But I don't slur.

Tape yourself sometime and you'll see. Tapes don't lie.

So, she'd done just that and played it many times, but she didn't hear any slurred words but did notice that she sounded odd but she couldn't quite place how. She played it for her voice coach, and she said that she saw the problem right away.

You're saying everything from your mouth. There is no depth, no resonance in your voice. Practice talking more from your chest cavity.

Isn't that more for singers? she'd asked.

It is true that singers must learn to sing from their diaphragm and not their throat. But you're not a singer and I didn't say diaphragm.

None of the five people she'd loved had ever said anything about the way she spoke, and they certainly didn't say that she slurred her words. The most recent, Ryan, had asked her to repeat things a few times but she blamed that on his poor hearing in this left ear due to a childhood illness. He said he liked the sound of her voice and that at times she sounded melodic and seemed on the verge of singing and he sometimes expected her to burst into song but she never did and he thanked her for that, the one time they spoke after they broke up.

Don't take it so hard. With the right practice you will be fine. We all change in ways as we age. This is being done for you.

For me?

Yes, for you. That is always the best way to think of such matters. I'd heard someone say that once and it's stuck with me. It's how I've lived my life since.

Yeah right, she'd thought but never said and was glad now that she hadn't because she continued to see her voice coach and was sensing progress. The practicing in front of the mirror was helping her as was thinking about the correct placement of her tongue in her mouth.

She did realize that saying certain sounds more slowly caused the meaning to be suspended and even dropped for her. She's played her recordings many times and still didn't hear herself slur any words. In fact, she thought that she enunciates more carefully than most people at work, and she attributed that to all her practicing.

She had worried in the beginning that this was the start of something worse. A warning sign, like a stutter, and that in time she would misplace all her vowels and then the consonance one by one. But her voice coach had assured her that wouldn't happen and that this was but a glitch and not the beginning of a decline.

A few months later, Marsha took a job in the land office of another oil company a block from where Janice worked and no longer was her supervisor. Her new supervisor hadn't complained once about her slurring her words or called her into his office. He seemed more detached from the day-to-day duties of the department than Marsha. He had an accent too that indicated that English was not his first language. She understood him just fine. Whenever she passed his office, his door was always open, and he was typing on his laptop. He rarely looked up or glanced in her direction. She was certain now that in time his office would become hers. She also knew she would have practiced ample enough by then that she will no longer even misplaced vowels. That was how it all unified and then came apart. Unified and then came apart.

Tale of the Crescent Wrench

Hand me the crescent wrench, his father said. They were in the garage and his father was leaning under the open hood of the Studebaker. *It was his pride and joy* he'd said numerous times at the dinner table. Roger didn't really know how to take that as he'd done enough reading by then to know that a Studebaker was not a very good car. It had a lot of factory defects, and the company wasn't doing very well. He wished his father would have bought a Chrysler or even A Chevy, but he'd fallen in love with the 1956 Studebaker. Once he stepped in the car showroom at the Studebaker dealer in Winnipeg there was nothing that Roger could say to his father to convince him to just walk away. Roger knew he'd be the one driving it on evenings and weekends even though most of his friends wouldn't be caught dead riding in a *Studebaker.*

No Way, they'd all said. Brian and Dave still went with him but they both said they preferred the back seat, so he had to sit up front alone. They'd stop at the *A & W* and then later at *The Cecil Cafe* in town. They weren't old enough to buy alcohol or get into the any of the bars in town besides everyone knew his father as he was the chief of police, so Roger had to be on his best behavior.

He had a plan to leave home at eighteen and go to university in Vancouver as that was as nearly far west that he could go in Canada. There was still Victoria, but he'd read that it was a city for old people. He never once considered going east.

When he was alone in his room, he'd have the radio on and be reading a teen magazine and or a book. He particularly liked

Mad Magazine because it made him laugh. He especially like *Spy Vs Spy*. When he was younger, he liked comics like *Archie* and *Superman*. Because of the Archie comics he'd dreamed of having a hot rod, but he didn't read them anymore and the Studebaker would have to do.

The bigger crescent wrench, his father said now. That one was a foot long and Roger lifted it off its hook on the wall of the garage. It was meant for large nuts so meant that his father was needing to do some serious fiddling under the hood. This didn't surprise Roger as even though the Studebaker wasn't very old. It often needed tweaking and tuning.

His father tapped metal a couple of times with the wrench and then used it to open the master cylinder. *Hand me the can of brake fluid from that shelf over there.* He pointed to metal shelves on the left side of the garage. Roger already knew where the fluid was and got the can and twisted off the metal cap and passed the can to his father.

He knew from his reading that a car this new shouldn't need to have the brake fluid topped up. *Is it leaking?* he asked.

Some his father said and then *maybe.* His father always defended the Studebaker no matter who disparaged it.

Maybe wasn't definitive enough of an answer for Roger. He stepped back from the car and walked around it and peered under each wheel wall to look for signs of a brake line leak but saw none. But the fluid had to be going somewhere. He asked his father about that.

It happens sometimes. That's cars. They need their fluid topped up. His father said that as though to teach his son about the maintenance of cars. But Roger studied auto shop at school and his teacher had already said that new cars didn't leak fluids and that leaking fluids of any kind were a bad sign especially in a new car.

The next time he drove the car he pumped the brakes several times at the end of the block, and they grabbed high in the pedal, so he accepted that maybe this time his father was right. Still that night when he got home from driving around town with his friends, he popped the hood and took the foot-long crescent wrench off the hook on the wall. He loosened the bolt on the master cylinder enough that he could twist it off the rest of the way with his fingers. He looked inside the cylinder and it was full. He took that as a good sign and that his father had been right.

The following Saturday he was out with his friends again. This time Wanda, Dave's younger sister was sitting in the front. She had just turned sixteen and said she wanted to come along for the ride when he picked up Dave. She chewed gum and fiddled with the radio, but he didn't say anything because he liked her, but that was as far as he would go given that she was two years younger than him. He was a bit nervous with her in the car and took extra care around the corners. At the one stoplight, at Second Street and Main Street, he was driving west so stopped at the right-hand lane. A hot rod like the one in the Archie comics, except it was a sky blue instead of red and more souped up than Archie's, pulled up beside his car in the left lane. The driver revved the engine, and it had a rumble to it that the Studebaker couldn't match so he didn't bother to rev it. Nor did he look to his left to see who was driving or in the car. He'd never seen the hot rod before so that meant it likely came from Winnipeg for the day. Like the car in the Archie comics, it was from a couple of decades back with no cover over the engine. It had no hood and was a four-seater.

There's Archie, Wanda said and pointed in the direction of the car. The engine revved again, and this time Roger glanced over, and the driver waved. A friendly wave and the passenger in the front waved too and then giggled. He heard someone shout, *Hey Studebaker,* and in that moment, he took his father's side and was proud of the car was glad he was driving the Studebaker and not the hot rod. Wanda turned up the radio and *Splish Splash,* his favourite song so far for 1958, played loud throughout the car. The hot rod found the same station and turned up the song even louder. and the song rang out into the street. He then shifted his gaze to the few pedestrians waiting for the light to change and he expected to them to be moving just a bit to the beat, but they were his father's age and they remained still as they waited for the light to change.

Wanda bobbed her head to the beat and Brian and Dave did the same in the back seat. Roger tapped the steering wheel and the driver of the hot rod whistled and Roger turned that way, and he flashed a thumbs up and then tapped his steering wheel too.

The light changed then the hot rod squealed its tires and sped through the intersection and then braked hard for the quick dip to the back street next to the lake. Roger turned right but waited for the pedestrians to cross first and then eased down the block barely accelerating the car. The radio continued to play loud and then the song ended. At the end of the first block the hot rod emerged from the direction of the lake and waited for Roger and the Studebaker to pass then it turned behind them.

How sweet, Wanda said looking behind. *Rave On* played next and Roger heard it echoing behind him. When he checked the rear- view mirror, he saw that the hot rod had Manitoba plates. He slowed the Studebaker and tried the brakes out of habit, and they were fine. Th driver of the hot rod pulled out into the left lane then and came alongside his car. The driver revved the engine so he must have put the clutch in and let the car glide. That's how slow Roger was driving. The next lights were at the railway underpass. Both cars stopped there and now *Good Golly Miss Molly* was playing and the hot rod turned that even louder and the driver didn't rev the engine.

Go Wanda said as soon as the light turned green. He touched the gas enough that the Studebaker squealed its rear tires on the right turn under the overpass. The hot rod went straight in the direction of Winnipeg. The song faded under the overpass, and he realized at some point he'd turned down the radio. Both Brian and Dave were leaning forward in the back seat and Dave said, *Cool* at him squealing the tires. *Yeah Cool,* Wanda said. He slowed through the windy streets toward the papermill. He realized then he wasn't going anywhere just driving in the fading light of a summer's day even though it was close to 10 pm. He thought about that hot rod and the windy drive back to Winnipeg with the hood down. Even with the radio turned way up it would be barely audible with all that wind noise.

He was at the top of the hill now just above the papermill and he tried the brakes and he had none. He pumped them again but nothing. He said nothing to anyone else in the car. He geared down to first gear and Brian pushed closer to him as though to let him know he knew what was going on. Wanda was looking straight ahead. *Good Golly, Miss Molly* finished now and there was an ad for

Campbell's Furniture and RCA TVs and then an ad for the Shop Easy in town. They were having a sale. But they had a sale every week he was thinking and then pulled out the hand brake from beneath the steering wheel. This caused Wanda to look in his direction. The engine roared but the engine compression held on the hill and with that and the hand brake the car slowed and then stopped up the slight incline at the papermill. He stopped there and then turned left toward the employee parking lot and stayed in first gear and then used the parking brake when he pulled into a free space next to a red Dodge half-ton.

He turned the engine off and got out. Wanda got out and stood next then her brother and Brian. They looked at the car and then at Roger and Wanda said, *savvy.*

Yeah savvy, her brother said and that was it.

They walked toward the papermill where there'd be a phone and he would call his father at the police station to send someone to pick them up. His father was going to be pissed, not at him nor at the Studebaker, but at the fact that there had been a leak. He played back in his mind his looking under the hood and tightening the bolt on the master cylinder with the crescent wrench. He knew he tightened it fine. Maybe not as tight as his father had but tight enough. He was certain that wasn't the problem but wouldn't dare look under the hood to check.

Tale of the For Sale Sign

JAN USES THE LOCKBOX TO LET HERSELF IN. SHE'S AT LEAST A HALF hour early, but she prefers it that way as it allows her to do another walk through and remind herself of the high points of a given property. These days that isn't required as houses in the Point Grey area of Vancouver practically sell themselves and most properties sell at a premium even in a slower market like now. The owners have recently had the pool in the back redone and the front entrance way now has a black slate floor. She sold this very house ten year ago and then it had been very different. A typical west coast bungalow from the 1970s with a lot of browns and carpet everywhere. Now there isn't any carpet. Mostly there's hardwood. Oak and maple and then in the den some teak. She isn't sure about that because even though teak is rarer and more expensive it isn't to everyone's taste. The current owners are both real estate lawyers who will be doing their own contracts for the purchase.

The owners Randy and Kim are not her clients, and this isn't her listing, but the potential buyers are hers. They're a retired couple from Toronto. She was a dentist, and he was a broker at least that is what they've told her. They plan to buy a house outright as they had a decent house in Toronto that has already sold. They want to retire to the west coast. *Walk along the sea wall,* Debbie had said when they first came into her office and asked to be shown around. Stephen didn't talk much and used his cell phone a lot. *He's still active. I'm done.* Is how Debbie put it.

She's shown them videos of five properties and this one and another house in Kerrisdale are the ones they've asked to see. Debbie has struck her as the smarter one who likely made the decisions and Stephen went along with her and likely that's worked out well for them. Debbie has told her that the house they owned in Toronto she'd inherited from her parents because she was an only child. Her parents had been the salt of the earth she'd said. They'd own a hardware store but ended up selling out to Home Hardware two decades ago.

Randy and Kim have done a great job of straightening up and although she's done a full walk through, nothing has needed adjusting. She's in the living room now going over the spec sheet. The living room window has a tiny glimpse of the harbor at least she thinks it's the harbor, but it is a bit hard to tell with all the morning glare off the various buildings. It's blue that's all she knows for certain, and it's not sky blue.

Debbie and Stephen pull up then, and she watches the Mercedes park itself. She's mesmerized how cars can do that now. Debbie is behind the wheel, and she gets out first and shields her eyes as she looks up at the second story of the house. Her hair is shorter than it was when they sat in her office and red now although it had been blonde that day. Stephen is wearing a wool hat and because of the angle of it, at first, she thinks it's a beret and that he looks slightly French but as he moves towards the house and she gets a better look and sees that in fact he's wearing a tweed peeked hat like they wear in Scotland. She wonders if his family is Scottish or Irish?

Not a single thing about him has struck her as being Scottish or Irish.

The doorbell rings and she answers it.

Debbie is standing slightly in front of Stephen and reaches out a hand for her to shake. *I love the outside. Don't you Stephen?* she says.

Yes, he says and immediately has his cell phone out. He pokes at it a couple of times and then puts it away again.

Save that for later, Debbie says, and he nods. *What year was it build?*

1968 but it's been updated Jan says. *I can show you the pictures from before,* she says.

That won't be necessary. This entrance way is just lovely. Slate right? Debbie says.

Yes slate. They had that put in last summer. There's slate in the main floor bathroom too and terracotta tile upstairs and oak.

Lovely, Debbie says. She goes to the main bathroom now. And pokes her head inside but doesn't go all the way inside. *Lovely* she says then. *Is it okay if we just walk around by ourselves? We prefer it that way.*

This is unusual as Jan likes the point out the various features of the property, but if this is what her clients want she's learned to be agreeable.

She hears them upstairs moving from room to room. They don't stop in any one room for long. She keeps a mental image of each room in her head and tries to anticipate which features they'll like and which they won't. She usually has a pretty good read on clients by this time, but sometimes they surprise her too and she has a feeling that the Stephen and Debbie will surprise her.

Stephen comes downstairs by himself and nods at her and then walks to the door to the basement and goes on down there. Debbie stays upstairs a long time although Jan no longer hears her moving about. She wonders what this all means. Usually her clients stick together, and couples tend to talk a lot which helps her understand what they like and don't like about a given property but Stephen and Debbie are unusually quiet. She has begun to wonder just how suited they are as couple as Debbie seems keen and highly engaged while Stephen seems aloof and distant. Given his behavior, Jan would have thought he was the one who inherited a bit of wealth more than Debbie, but people come in all shapes and sizes and pigeon holing them in her line of work is a guarantee to failure.

Stephen doesn't come back upstairs, and Debbie doesn't come downstairs. She waits for twenty minutes and there's no sign of either of them. By now she knows she should check them but who does she check out first? She decides that Debbie is the best choice. She goes upstairs moving as quiet as possible and wonders why she is doing that, but she is.

She doesn't find Debbie at first and considers calling out to her but decides that would seem strange. She finds Debbie sitting on the bed in what had been Randy and Kim's son's room. She's crying.

That shit, she says when Jan comes into the room. Jan doesn't say anything although she knows that Debbie must mean Stephen as she can't imagine who else Debbie could be talking about.

Are you alright? That shit.

What happened?

The usual. That shit.

Are you going to be okay?

He wants everything taken out. Even the tile. Where is he? In the basement.

Sure. What's down there?

Games room, home theatre, fitness room, and another bathroom.

That's him.

Should we move onto to the next house?

No this will do. I'm not ripping out any tile though. I'm okay. I'll be down in a bit.

Okay. Jan leaves her here and returns to the living room. She expects Stephen to be back up by now, and she goes through every room on the main floor, but he's not in any of them. She takes an extra-long inhale and then goes to the basement. It's a walk out basement on the east side where the pool is and has French doors facing the pool. They are still open as she left them. She goes to the games room first and then the home theatre, but Stephen isn't in either. She searches the entire basement, but he isn't anywhere. She goes back to the French doors to see if he's gone out to the pool but he's not there either. She closes those doors and goes back upstairs and at the front windows she sees him sitting behind in the driver's seat of the Mercedes.

She isn't quite sure what to make of this so stays in the living room going through the spec sheet ten more times. Debbie finally comes downstairs and says, *Thank you,* and goes out the front door and down the walk way to the Mercedes. Not once does she look back at the house. She gets in the passenger car and sits there. She is looking straight ahead, and they don't appear to be talking.

Jan moves to the leather love seat that has an even better view of the Mercedes. Nothing like this has ever happened in the twenty- years plus years she has been selling real estate. She doesn't have an idea of what to do.

Fifteen minutes later her cell phone rings. It's Debbie. *Hi*, she says. Her voice sounds so neutral as though nothing out of the ordinary has happened. *We'd like to see the other house now* she says and then says goodbye and hangs up.

Tale of the Skeleton Key

THE YEAR IS 1944, AND SHE KEEPS THE SKELETON KEY IN HER SMALL hand purse with the wooden clasp. She uses it twice a day. Once in the morning when she leaves for work and then again just before dinner when she returns home from work. Her room is on the third floor of the boarding house and Mrs. Anderson is always sweet to her. Mrs. Anderson lost her husband in the first world war. She didn't have the boarding house then. That came later after her father died and left her a large enough sum that she could purchase the house. She calls Alice, Miss Sharpe, and calls everyone at the dinner table as either Mr. or Miss. There is no Mrs., except for Mrs. Anderson. There's not even a single widow. She doesn't rent to widows she has told Alice.

The meals are ample, and Alice has no complaints that way and is always full when she leaves for work and full again after dinner. She takes a small sandwich with her to work and eats that with Roz and Winnie in the lunchroom. The three of them sit at the same table and by now know each other's story very well at least the parts they've told. Alice has never been in love, grew up on a farm, has strict and loving parents that she writes to at least once a week. Always to her mother and her mother writes back mostly about herself but saves space at the end of each letter to mention her father. She signs the letters, *Your mother,* and Alice signs hers, *your daughter.* That part is easy because she only has two brothers and no sisters. Her brothers both help on the farm and live in the farmhouse. They don't have any interest in Winnipeg. Her mother has stressed that in early letters, but she hasn't mentioned it recently. Winnie and Roz know that much about her, but she's never told them about the two young men she dated before moving to the city. They had been farmers.

Grant was a bit older than her and already had a farm of his own and said he wanted her to be his wife, but he never said what that meant so she didn't agree. Besides she didn't really love him as he had a habit of laughing when something wasn't funny. She knew he did that out of nervousness but that had been the point.

Dale, the other man, she'd dated during her last year of high school. He had escorted her to a dance at the high school. He'd graduated the year before her and helped his father on their farm. His parents had a large wheat farm with so many acres it took an hour to drive the perimeter in his half-ton. Dale talked a lot. Mostly about the farm and the future of the farm and about grain prices and now and then about cows as they had a dozen milking cows.

He never mentioned marriage but was angling toward it she could tell. He'd since married a woman from town, and they had a son now. Alice ran into them twice when she had been back visiting her parent's farm near Beausejour. Grant never got married but died recently overseas in the war.

There are a couple of appealing men staying at the boarding house, but they are much older because of the war. She's had stimulating conversations with each over dinner, but she always gets up first and goes back to her room. She doesn't lock her room when she comes down for meals so doesn't need the skeleton key then. After dinner she usually reads. Novels mostly from the last century.

Novels from a time when there was no war, and people fell in and out of love without all the foreboding that had.

After breakfast, she takes the streetcar to the small arms munition factory near the airport. The war has made it easier for her to come to the city and get a job. She could be thankful about that but she's not. In her first job she sorted through the brass casings looking for any bad ones and then fed each good one down the line. Later she was moved between Winnie and Roz.

They have to wrap their hair in cloth for work so with her first pay cheque she'd bought a half dozen of them and hand washes them on Sundays in the bathroom sink down the hall.

Winnie adds the primer to the bottom of each casing. She uses a die for this and that must be seated just right, or the bullet won't fire. She then passes the casing and die to Alice and she adds the propellent. This is brown strands of cordite that resemble strands of straw. As she does this, she doesn't think about how dangerous this is. If she did, she would lose her nerve and walk away.

Winnie, Roz, and she have talked about how it is important not to think about the dangers of what they are doing and to just do the job. *It is for the war effort.*

Alice adds 2.4 oz of cordite strands to each casing and then passes the casing and die to Roz who inserts the aluminum pointed bullet on top and taps it down until it is properly seated. By then Winnie has passed another casing and die to Alice to fill. When Roz releases the loaded bullet from the die, it is armed. She passes it to another woman, Debra, who inspects each bullet to make sure they've got it right. Just yesterday she complimented them saying that they did the best work and that very few of their bullets were rejected. There is a range at the other end of the factory where samples of the bullets are fired to make sure they work properly.

Before she got this job, she never looked at a bullet. Her brothers had been the ones drawn to guns and hunting. Now sometimes as she's filling a casing she wonders about the bullet and where it will end up and whether it will it serve the soldier well in battle. When she was in high school, she'd learned about the first world war in history class and knew that another war was brewing but now that she worked in this factory, she realizes that wars are fought with many different weapons some requiring the three of them to load bullets for battles fought far away.

She returns home tonight and takes the skeleton key out of her purse and unlocks her door. As he does, Mr. Talbot passes in the hall. He limps because of a bad fall off a horse on the farm when he was thirteen. She has only spoken to him once because he always sits at the far end of the table from her and next to Mrs. Anderson. His room is next to hers and she watches him take out a similar skeleton key and place it in the lock and unlocks his door. He turns towards her then. He is only a couple of years older than her, but his smile at this moment makes him look much older and more burdened. She would normally turn away from him and go into her room and wash in the basin she has filled in the morning for that purpose, but she stays facing him and asks after his day.

He says it has been fine like most.

He works as a clerk for the Hudson Bay store. He hasn't told her that, but Mrs. Anderson did when she moved in. She gave Alice a quick summary of each tenant. Alice has often wondered since what Mrs. Anderson tells others about her, but as she thinks about that now she realizes it doesn't matter as it won't be true. That causes her to wonder if what she has told her about Mr. Talbot's accident is true. She has heard about men maiming themselves to get out of war. She wonders how anyone could do that given how much it would likely hurt. She decides then that Mr. Talbot really did fall from a horse when he was thirteen.

He hasn't gone in his room but holds the door half open. He asks her about her day, and she says she can't really talk about it which is her way of saying that she is serving the war effort. He nods for everyone knows the meaning of that. Likely Mrs. Anderson has told him that much. His hair is slicked back with something oily but that makes his face dominate. He is more handsome than either Grant or Dale and his red hair is a dark red. He has a lot of freckles on his face which means at some point he has spent a lot of time in the sun, and she imagines that he returns home to the family farm often like her.

She doesn't know what direction his farm is from Winnipeg but has an immediate feeling that it is west of the city in the direction of Portage la Prairie. She doesn't ask him that now as that likely will come up later. She imagines after today that he will shift his position at the dinner table to be closer to her. Not right beside her as that would be too presumptuous but closer and they will talk more.

He holds the doorknob with his right arm and leans on it likely to take some of the pressure off his left leg. She hasn't noticed him do that before but assumes he must do it often and senses that he feels pain with every step. She doesn't know what that feels like except after a long day of filling ammunition her fingers burn and her neck and shoulders ache. Some of the women at the factory are older like, Debra, and they often complain of pain and how the long hours wear on them. She hopes the war ends soon as she doesn't wish to be doing this work indefinitely. As soon as she thinks that she admonishes herself because she hears how selfish it sounds.

My brothers are overseas, Mr. Talbot says now, and she recognizes pride in the smile he flashes.

Mine are working on the farm, she says.

Right, he says and moves the door slightly back and forth on its hinges.

She's not sure what that means except perhaps boredom. She doesn't know what she should ask about his brothers so asks, *Do you hear from them often?*

Every few weeks Mom gets a letter. One is in Britain. The other is in France. We hear from Charles, the one in France, the most often.

Normandy? Yes.

That was a few months ago now.

I hear you at night, he says. *Your chair on the floor.*

Yes, the walls are thin. She's heard him limp from his table to the bed and back but doesn't mention that.

Your horse? she asks and wishes she hadn't brought that up.

It rose up because of a fox on the trail. Luckily Charles was with me and rode me back to the farm and went to town for the doctor. The doctor set it at the farm but said because of the break I won't walk normal. He got that part right. If it weren't for Charles, it would have been much worse.

You must miss him?

Yes, terribly so. I read his letters through many times. He's a much better letter writer than my brother Frank. His letters are always so short. He ends up with the choice assignments. Charles on the other hand likes to tough it out.

She doesn't tell him, but she senses already that Charles won't make it home, but Frank will. That thought makes her sad even though she doesn't know either of them. But based on Mr. Talbot she assumes they were raised well.

I've enjoyed this conversation she says and opens her door. It opens out opposite to his so she can hold it open and still see him.

I have too, he says. He doesn't go in but continues to stand there.

She nods at him and goes in first and pulls her door closed. She waits to hear him close his, but he doesn't do that for a full minute. She almost opens her door to see what has caused the delay, but she doesn't risk it. Finally, she hears it shut and he closes it much quieter than she had, and she doesn't hear anything until the final latching.

She goes to the wall that they have in common and puts an ear to it. She has never done this before. She listens to him limp first closer to her wall then away from it and toward where his bed is. She hasn't seen his room but assumes it has similar layout to hers. She hears what sounds like mattress springs and she imagines him lying on his bed with his hands behind his head. Thinking. She lies on her bed and does the same and all she can think about is Charles riding Mr. Talbot to safety. She has no idea what Charles looks like, so gives him a face like Mr. Talbot's, except that Mr. Talbot's face is more complete. She thinks about his face now and imagines his brother carrying him. He's not smiling like today, and his eyes are closed and that means he is coping with the pain with each gallop of the horse.

She naps but wakes in time for dinner. She gets up and fixes her hair in the mirror and then goes out without locking her door and goes downstairs. Mr. Talbot doesn't come down to dinner. She asks Mrs. Anderson about this later and she says he sometimes does that when he's tired from work and that she will later bring him up a plate.

Tale of the Rusted Chimes

ALBERT HEARD THE CHIMES FOR THE FIRST TIME THE DAY AFTER Karen and he moved into the house. He hadn't noticed them when Karen and he viewed the house nor when they did a second walk through before making the offer.

The first night, after they'd worked hard all day to unpack everything, they'd both fallen asleep quickly in their bed. He remembered his last thought that day was how good it felt knowing that there was an old oak tree was just outside the bedroom window. But sometime in the middle of the night a wind must have picked up and a terrible rattle woke him. It was such an abrasive noise that he bolted upright in bed straight out of a dream and assumed the racket was part of the dream that that had woken him. But as he sat beside Karen in bed, he heard the racket again and this time Karen woke too and sat up and he knew she'd heard it too.

What is that? She'd asked.

I don't know. He said, *Maybe, something has gotten caught in the tree or gathered along by the wind and once the wind dies down the noise will stop.*

Maybe, she'd said and as soon as she said it the racket was so loud that they both covered their ears.

It's like nails on a chalkboard, she'd said.

Yes, he'd said.

Neither got out of bed but they waited side-by-side and in time the wind did die down and the noise stopped, and he thought that was the end of it.

He slept well for the rest of the night and woke feeling fresh and delighted to be waking in their new house.

They both dressed, had breakfast, and hurried off to their separate jobs and he soon forgot about the racket and assumed it was some mysterious noise caused the wind.

When they each returned home from work that day, they ate dinner in the circular alcove off the kitchen that they both liked. He'd sautéed a salmon fillet and she'd chopped a plentiful garden salad. They ate solely and bubbled to each other about how lovely their new house was.

That night they slept without incident, and both soon forgot about the terrible racket that had so unceremoniously woken them on their first night here.

It wasn't until the weekend of their first week in the house that the racket returned. This time they had made love as they often did on Friday evenings taking their time. He fell asleep quickly soon after and then woke late into the night to the same racket only this time it was much louder, so loud he first thought upon waking that the sound was coming from inside the house. There was a strong wind again and each time the wind picked up the racket built to a crescendo and didn't let up. Karen soon woke and said, *Again?*

Again, he said.

This time they both laid back down and he tried not to listen. He held Karen and her breathing close to his ear soothed him and despite the racket he was some place good.

It's outside, right? She said.

Yes outside. I thought at first inside. It was so loud, but it is outside. And related to the wind? Yes related to the wind.

They cuddled then and when the wind slowed, and the racket quieted and that ceased she turned her back to him and he spooned behind her and felt the rise and fall of her breathing and he said to himself how happy he was here with her.

The next day was Saturday, so they were up early, and he took down the ten-foot ladder from the garage and carried it to the back of the house and together they inspected the outside of the house first. The siding was painted oak shakes and not a single one of them had come loose in fact the previous owners had recently had every shake properly secured so not a single one of them were loose.

He then turned his attention to that massive, beautiful oak next to the house. When they first viewed the house, they both professed love for this massive oak just outside the bedroom window. Albert had felt the oak made the house more romantic.

He moved the ladder to it now and climbed to the top of the ladder as Karen supported the base. It was then that he saw the chimes tucked under a large leafy branch. He was high enough to see how repulsive and rusted they were. He could see that the chimes had been secured by a thick wire wrapped around the branch. That must have been done to withstand the strongest of winds.

The chimes were a rusted assortment of ancient knives and forks that looked like they came from two centuries ago it was them striking each other that made the frightful metal sound that sounded like the dangling rusted flatware that they were.

The chimes looked so worn and rusted that he doubted that the previous owners, the Cranes, had put it up there. He assumed a previous owner from them had lodged the chimes there and it had stayed there all these years.

When he climbed back down, Karen asked them how they could get rid of it.

It's too high for me to reach so we'll have to call someone. An arborist or at least a tree trimmer. Someone with a truck with a hoist and a bucket.

After that he got out the yellow pages and went to the appropriate section. He assumed in no time he would have it taken care of. It was a Saturday so many of the numbers went to voice mail. It wasn't until the sixth number that he got an answer. The voice that answered was gruff and sound liked someone who smoked a lot of cigars or drank a lot of whisky or both. His name was Bruce, and he was an arborist and he sound excited to receive the call until he learned that Albert didn't need the tree trimmed only a chimes removed.

A chimes? Bruce said and then laughed, and his laugh was even gruffer and more guttural than his voice. *Can't you just climb up and take it out. I can't come out for a small job like that.*

I'll pay you well.

I'm fully booked at the moment. I've got a lot of big jobs ahead of you. It will be three weeks or a month before I can get to you.

Three weeks? Can't you just slip us in. It won't take that long. That's the point. The job is too small. He hung up even then.

Albert called back twice but got a busy tone each time so took the hint. He tried too more places but got no answers.

He realized that he might have to wait until Monday and call from work. *What about hiring a student to go up there,* Karen suggested. *If the student were to fall and get injured, we'd have all the liabilities. I am sure I'll find someone on Monday. Someone will do it for the right amount of money.*

That night and Sunday night there was no wind and so Albert and Karen both slept through the night. He woke on Monday before Karen and showered and dressed and then fixed them both coffees. He used to like the view of the oak from the alcove but today he couldn't stand to look at it and instead sat with his back to it and so had a drab view of the street out front. Karen came down when he was half finished his coffee and sat on the same side as him with her back to the oak.

At work he started at the first number on the list again and this time a woman answered. She said she was just the service and booked appointments. He said what he needed done and she said she couldn't book an appoint for something that small. He tried two more and go similar replies so for the third one he said he wanted an appointment to have the oak trimmed. This worked and he had someone coming out on Friday. He'd have to take that day off work, but he'd put in so many extra hours that wouldn't be a problem.

Karen was very pleased when she got home and told him that he was very clever to have booked a tree trim because even though the tree didn't really need it that would get someone out and the monstrosity soon gone.

On the Friday he stayed home and the tree trimming truck showed up right on time at ten am. The driver of the truck was a pleasant young man named Hans. When Albert pointed out the wind chimes that he wanted taken down instead, Hans' tone changed.

I'm here to trim an oak tree. I can take down the chimes, but I've got to trim the tree too. My boss requires me to take photos to show that I've done a proper job. I have to charge the full fee too. I have to do the trim.

But the tree doesn't need a trim. You can see that. It was done recently by the previous owners. Another trim now might ruin it.

I'll be careful but I've got to trim it so I can take before and after photos. Hans produced a cell phone and took three pictures of the tree from various angles including from below and from far away on both sides. He then went to his truck and got into the bucket and raised the arm first high into the left main branch of the tree and cut it back ten feet. He then went to the right main branch and cut it back ten feet as well. He worked his way down the tree until he got to the wind chimes. Then he took a long time with plyers and metal cutters to snap it free from the tree. When he finally released it the chimes fell straight down into the grass and when it was safe Alberta wore leather gardening gloves and ran and collected it and carried it by pinching one of the spoons between his gloved thumb and forefinger. He hurried it to the garbage bins at the back of the yard.

When Hans was done the tree looked skeletal and about half the size it had been. Albert couldn't believe how bare and vulnerable it looked. When he went inside to the bedroom it was much brighter as the removed branches had shaded that side of the house. He knew Karen wouldn't be at pleased by that, but the chimes were gone.

He paid Hans in cash and then Hans took four pictures this time. Two from below and two from far away. He then thanked Albert for the work and gave him a detailed receipt and climbed into the cab of his truck and drove away.

Karen squealed when she came home. He was at the alcove then looking at the oak and wondering how a tree could have caused him to love this house. She squealed not once but twice and that told him the mood she would be in when she came inside.

What happened? She asked as she tossed her keys on the table and sat on the same side of him looking at the tree.

He told her everything and explained again how it was the only way to get the chimes down.

But the tree looks so butchered. It's less than half its size.

It'll grow back. Paring a tree way back is good for it. Hans said.

She didn't respond but looked in the direction of the tree and he knew she felt the same he did. That the house was just not the same.

That night he didn't sleep at all. There was no annoying racket although the wind did pickup during the night as it tended to do on summer nights. He felt restless the whole night. In the morning, more light flooded in too and he had to get up after an hour and completely close the blinds, something he'd never had to do before. Oddly more than missing the branches cut from the tree, he missed those chimes. He could still conjure them up in his head and how rusted they were and how many years they had endured the elements there and what exactly had he done by having them ripped out of the tree and tossed in the trash. He'd worn gloves to make sure none of the rust touched him.

Tale of the Off Season

RED AND BURGUNDY SHELLS FLICK IN SUNLIGHT AND WATER ON THE beach and later a single crab floats for a time until the tide speeds up and then all of that vanishes in the swirling water. Above, a cloudless sky is a single shade of blue. Not the blue of water but the blue of air, of difficulty, of short breaths, and dive of a gull hungry for what churns in the busy water.

The dog runs along the beach and somewhere behind him the boy and behind him, the boy's mother. She's carrying a backpack slung loosely over one shoulder. They have left their red car, a recent model Suzuki, parked along the road, and have hurried to the beach. She has told him all about how as a girl she would wade into the icy water of this very bay and how the water was so cold her legs would go numb right away.

There's a song about this, Lisa tells him.

There is? Carl asks.

The dog has found something on the beach that he nuzzles pushing its head back and forth. This is not a trick the boy taught him but something always in the dog and only manifesting now. The boy calls the dog by his name, Blackie, but the dog doesn't stop what he's doing. This far away he could have come across anything. The boy can't imagine what it might be. He asks his mother.

Carrion, she says.

Carl has never heard that word before and isn't sure what it means and the first thing he thinks of is a rubber ball like the one he tosses for the dog in the back yard at home. Blackie loves to chase the ball, but the boy always tires of it first and goes inside. When he looks outside later, Blackie is usually nuzzling the ball.

What is carrion? he asks after another couple of steps.

Something dead, Lisa says finally. She is standing right behind him when she says this and then rests a hand on his shoulder, and he associates those words with her hand on his shoulder and how secure he feels in this moment. She could have told him anything and it would have been fine.

The dog has managed to pick up the carrion and is running with it away from the boy and his mother. Whatever has died, looks at this distance like a black mass dangling from the dog's mouth as he runs.

Looks like a ling cod, Lisa says.

The boy has heard of ling cod and knows that people catch them off the islands in the Salish Sea, but he's never seen one or eaten one. He doesn't particularly like the taste of fish. *Too fishy* he's said whenever his mother has asked him why he doesn't like the taste.

How'd it die? he asks.

No way of knowing. Maybe it was sick or old or got smashed against the rocks by a big wave.

That can happen?

Yes.

The dog has stopped farther down the beach. There's a bit of wave action there as it isn't quite as protected from the wind, so the dog has moved the ling cod a bit further away from the water and into the sand. He drops the ling cod and appears to be eating it.

Should I stop Blackie?

Leave him be.

Will he get sick from that dead fish?

Blackie is hearty. He's never been sick. He knows what he can and can't eat. He's clever that way.

Carl has stopped walking as he doesn't want to get any closer to the dog and the dead fish. He knows the dead ling cod will smell bad and he's not sure he'd like to see its mangled shape either. He's lived around the ocean and beaches long enough to know that dead creatures that wash ashore are usually grey monstrosities blanched by water action. Any hint of the living parts of them are soaked out, so they no longer resemble the living creatures that they once were.

The fish will taste salty and foul and maybe that's what Blackie finds the most appealing. The dog takes three more bites and then lifts the carcass and carries it into the water. He wades in until the water touches his belly, which isn't that far. The dog watches the water for a moment and then drops the carcass in the water and wades ashore. Once he reaches the sand he bolts back toward the boy and his mother. He doesn't stop when he reaches them but runs right past and toward where the car is parked. The dog barks many times as he runs.

The boy watches the carcass of the ling cod bob on the water until he determines that it's floating into shore and not out to sea. That means the tide is still coming in. He knows in a half hour or so that the fish will be deposited again on the sandy shore. By then he and his mother and the dog will be back in the red car and driving home. Blackie will sit in the back seat panting the whole way and will smell not of carrion but of salty air and water.

At the house Carl will open the back door of the car and let Blackie out and his mother will have the front door of the house open by then already and gone inside. He will let the dog go in first and then he will shut the front door. The dog will have bolted to the back door wanting outside as soon as he gets inside. The boy is used to these patterns but today is the first time he's seen the dog attracted to carrion. He thinks of the dog carrying the dead ling cod in his mouth down the beach. In the past he's thought that he could be a dog and that he understands all the things his dog does, and he's imagined himself doing the same things. But he can't imagine running down the beach with a dead fish in his mouth and he knows in a split second that is a good thing and that it means that he's going to be just fine.

Tale of the Future

HE'D DREAMED OF THE FUTURE OFTEN AND HE WAS NEVER IN THOSE dreams even though he knew he was one the dreaming them. Instead, he watched people go about his dream as they always did: purposeless or worse angry and troubled, picking fights with anyone they encountered. He would force himself to wake from such dreams but each time he'd wake under the same railway bridge. Nearby he'd hear rushing water, and if he got up and walked around, he'd smell dead fish and garbage.

Once when he closed his eyes and fell asleep, he had a very different dream. He was in that one. He was in a classroom but not like any classroom he'd ever been in. In one corner a fire burned in a barrel and in another a man or woman played a violin. Slow painful violin music and not the fiddle music he'd heard at home whenever his mother put on a record. He wondered about how the same instrument could be a violin or fiddle depending upon how it was played. The teacher in the classroom had long dirty hair and looked homeless and his hands were dirty, and he wrote on a blackboard that was out in the open. There were no walls anywhere.

The teacher taught a lesson about the difference between arteries and veins. He drew an elaborate image of a heart on the blackboard, and as soon as he finished the drawing, the heart started beating. He said, *This is your heart right now. You might think it is keeping time but in fact it is keeping you alive every second. It takes blood in and pumps it back out and that seems simple but what it is really doing is holding your soul in place, so you don't fly apart and cease to exist.*

71

He sat cross legged on damp ground in front of the blackboard and he could feel his pants soaking through, but he blocked that out and kept his eyes on the pumping heart. The teacher asked at this point if anyone had questions, and Ron raised his hand and asked:

How come the heart has four chambers. Who decided that? The teacher said that Ron was clever for asking that question and then said the heart evolved and once it developed four chambers it seemed to work best.

Think of the two-stroke engine and then the four-stroke engine. The later wouldn't exist without the former and yet the performance benefit from the change is significant. Nature works the same way. He didn't believe the teacher and didn't understand the difference between two and four-stroke engines, although he did know it was an allegory, but he wasn't what it was an allegory of.

When he woke, he was under the railway bridge but knew then that the allegory in his dream meant that in the future he would be a famous singer.

Your heart is making you one beat at a time. He remembered the teacher saying. A woman walked past where he lay and hummed a song that he would write a few years from now. He waited until she was gone and then he got up from where he'd slept and headed downtown where his friends waited. With their help, in a few hours he'd write a very important song.

Tale of the Half Acre

THE HORSE GRAZES BY THE NORTH GATE AS IT DOES EVERY MORNING. Her thoughts are horse thoughts which means a scrambled approximation of escape. But mixed in with that is a marvel at the full presence each day assumes. The corral is a fenced, square half acre with trees on three sides. The trees are ancient oaks that are robust but gnarly in the way oaks get when they are older and partly shaped by the elements. They lose their leaves like clockwork each fall and by winter their skeletal branches are aimed at an anemic sun.

The horse stays in the barn in winter, the farmer brings her a bag of wheat and oats each morning and again at night. There are three other horses in the barn. All male and older. Those horses were here when she arrived. The farmer calls her *Bright Challenge.*

That's the name she had when he bought her off the breeder. They had intended to race her, and she'd been very fast as a filly but slowed as a mare, but by then the name had stuck.

The girl who rides *Bright Challenge* is fourteen and has been riding her for two years. The girl is not here and hasn't ridden her in a month. The horse knows that the girl is sick and that is why she doesn't ride her. Today the farmer pushes the girl in a wheelchair and leaves her just outside the north gate as he does often. She has a blanket over her legs, and she watches *Bright Challenge* as she runs around the half acre corral and then grazes at the gate. Sometimes the girl brings an apple and offers it to the horse through the barb wire fence. The horse likes that part

73

and can always tell when the girl is about to bring out the apple because she smiles and then reaches into her coat pocket.

It is June and rains often but today it is not raining, and the girl is sitting by the gate. She has brought an apple and after the horse gulps down the apple the girl sings to her. The horse doesn't perceive it as a song or music but as the sounds the girl makes after giving her an apple. The horse does hear the girl sing *Bright Challenge* several times, but the rest of the song is but sounds that expand and converge all within the girl's voice. *How does she do that?* The horse wonders. The sounds the horse can make are not musical. Instead, she nickers or huffs or whinnies, or neighs or brays. Sharp, alarming, abrasive sounds that are more warnings or complaints than music. The horse doesn't really hear music, not even melodic chains of sounds. She hears the girl playing tricks with her breath.

Today the farmer brings a bucket of oats for the horse and opens the gate and leaves it on the ground for her. He then steps back behind the gate and locks it again and stands beside his daughter's wheelchair. The girl has stopped singing and won't sing as long as her father is there.

He thinks of how brave his daughter is because she is in pain most of the time now. The leukemia has a will of its own the doctor has warned him. All he can think about now is how happy *Bright Challenge* makes his daughter. She's always been around horses and took to them almost as soon as she could walk. Horses are different for him. They are big animals needing attention and affection more than most farm animals. They are not like mice or even dogs. They have visible egos and a pride and sometimes over confidence. *Bright Challenge* is overconfident. His daughter has said that is what she liked about *Bright Challenge, because the* horse's confidence had made her feel confident.

Being around *Bright Challenge* won't heal his daughter. Nothing will the doctor has made abundantly clear. The doctor has said that he perceives it as his duty not to allow the loved ones of his patients to get their hopes up. The farmer would prefer it if her doctor wasn't so pragmatic. He would like to pretend a bit and let his daughter pretend too. If she believed that *Bright*

Challenge could heal her, he would encourage her to believe it. But she doesn't. He hasn't told her much of what the doctor has told him, but he doesn't seem to need to as she seems to already sense that the end is near. Once she'd asked him, *Why*, and then later she said *I keep forgetting that I'm dying. Sometimes I wake in the morning with the nagging feeling that something's wrong, but at first, I don't know what it is and then I remember, Oh Yeah, I'm dying. I feel so terribly afraid then, but tell myself that it's not going to happen today.*

Bright Challenge is grey except for a large white spot on her nose and another even larger white spot on her right flank. When he bought her and brought her home to the farm his daughter had been healthy, and she'd smiled with such delight and then giggled so much that he'd felt a powerful tug of joy in his gut. She ran around the corral chasing *Bright Challenge*, and he'd thought in that moment how good life was. He clings to that feeling now and relives that memory often. That day, his daughter ran the full perimeter of the half acre twice without getting out of breath. The horse had been considerably faster than her and had stopped to wait for her to catch up several times. He'd thought, *that's something,* on that day and still does.

His daughter had been so happy that day that he'd brimmed with happiness too and he'd sensed how so very damn good and fine things could be. He felt his love for his daughter expand and broaden that day although he didn't know that was possible until it happened. By then his love for his daughter was already different from the love he felt for his wife.

But her illness has taught him another love beyond that. A deeper love partly at the cellular level and maybe deeper even than that. He doesn't really have a sense of what a cell contains except a nucleus and various cell materials. He senses though that what he feels for his daughter travels from cell to cell through his entirely in a different way than any other love has.

Recently he has started to dream backwards and wakes with the sensation that his daughter's illness has ceased to exist and that he's waking in a moment before all that, but of course he isn't. When his head clears ,and he realizes the truth, he admonishes himself for being taken in by such an illusion lasts because his daughter doesn't need illusions. She needs comforting and anchoring although he isn't certain how to anchor her or even what anchoring means other than bringing her out here to visit *Bright Challenge*.

Wheel me inside, she says now. *Bright Challenge* is still busy nuzzling the oats in the bucket. She lifts her head and whinnies once and then goes back to eating. When they get nearer, the horse lifts her head a second time and looks longer in their direction maybe uncertain what all of this is about.

I love the smell of her and of oats. I never knew that oats could smell so good. They smell green and earthy, his daughter says.

He remains behind her chair and doesn't answer because he doesn't really know what to make of what she's said. For weeks now he's concluded that she is hundreds of times smarter than him by now. Some of that comes from dying but mostly it comes from what's built into her. *That works the way it works,* he reminds himself. He knows about genetics and DNA, but he doesn't mean that. He loves his wife and together they made their daughter and now she is so very sick. He absentmindedly rests his thumb against his wrist and senses his pulse there. That causes him to recoil and immediately take his thumb away.

Bright Challenge has a pulse. He has a pulse. His daughter has a pulse. The triangulation of that ought to somehow calibrate a way to break out of this horrible shell that confines them. That will happen he knows but when the shell bursts his daughter will no longer be here.

Once she'd asked him, *what happens after?*

And he'd said, *I don't know.* Which is true but saying that to his daughter made him feel like such a failure.

I guess I'll find out, she'd said then. That that caught him off guard. Hearing those words coming from her seemed profane. His father had said something similar before he'd died but he'd been an old man and had been preparing to die for years.

Tell me a story, she says now, and for a second, he imagines she is saying this to the horse but of course she isn't.

He used to tell her stories when she was younger, but she'd grown out of that six years ago. He clears his throat and says without any hesitation: *There was a giant whose stride was half an acre long. In a single day he could walk a hundred miles.*

I wish there were giants, she says and that's her way of telling him that she has a different story in mind. Not one with giants or mice like the ones he told her when she was eight. *Tell me instead about Bright Challenge before she came here.*

He doesn't really know much about her before then. He'd bought her off a breeder and hadn't asked much about her except her temperament. The breeder had said she was a gentle horse and that had been what he had been looking for in terms of a horse for his daughter.

He tells her that *Bright Challenge had once been a wild horse that was born in the foothills south of Calgary and roamed from where the Bow River turns north to the range land to the south. When Bright Challenge was two, she and her herd disturbed a hibernating grizzly, and the bear woke mean and immediately charged the herd. The grizzly managed to claw Bright Challenge's mother and brought her down, but all the others got away. When the grizzly had eaten enough and slowed down and let the buzzards and foxes feast Bright Challenge came back and reared up and whinnied so fiercely that the bear ran off and so did all the others. Bright Challenge left then and returned to her herd.*

That's a brave horse, his daughter says.

Yes, she is brave. Like you.

I'm not brave. I'm afraid most of the time. But when I sit out here with Bright Challenge, and I look around this corral, it looks much bigger than half an acre. It looks like the largest and most expansive piece of land I've seen. I know that's false, but I like the feeling I get from thinking that.

He steps from behind the wheelchair and takes his daughter's hand, and she squeezes it and looks first at him and then at the horse that is now moving the bucket noisily along on the ground as it licks the last bit of oats.

I want to go back to the house now, his daughter says.

Alright, he says and let's go of her hand and goes behind the chair again and turns it around, and as he does, he turns her first toward *Bright Challenge* and then away. The horse nickers and comes a bit closer and then stops. He opens the gate and pushes his daughter through and then fastens the gate again. The horse doesn't come to the gate but stays where it is, gazing at his daughter.

Bye, his daughter says.

Bye, he says too and normally he'd feel foolish saying that to a horse but doesn't now.

The distance to the house is not far and most of the way is paved so it is easy to push the wheelchair. His daughter looks back several times in the direction of *Bright Challenge* but doesn't say anything. Both her hands stay beneath the blanket.

At the house he wheels her up the ramp he had put in for her months ago. *Stop,* she says when they are halfway up the ramp, so he stops. *Wait,* she says, so he waits. A few minutes later she says, *okay,* and he pushes her again toward the front door. Every moment of this is so very different from just two years ago when he brought *Bright Challenge* home. He turns his gaze then back toward that corralled half acre and he swears that the horse is looking in their direction but he's too far away to know for certain.

Tale of the Search Light

HE OPENS THE SLIDING GLASS DOOR OFF THE LIVING ROOM AND GOES outside and sits in a chair on the back deck. It's so dark he's invisible to anyone who might have a view the deck. *Hair,* the musical, is playing on the stereo behind him. He isn't certain why he is playing that except he hasn't listened to it in four decades.

Oddly the songs make perfect sense in the dark in ways they never have to him before. His wife slides open the glass door and sits in the chair next to him. All of this has been arranged earlier. She is naked like him and he reaches out his hand in the dark and she finds it and squeezes it.

It's not as chilly as I thought, she says and then asks, *can you find the Big Dipper.*

Will scans the night sky starting at his right and has to go clear across to his far left before he finds it. *There,* he says.

This is the first time they've ever sat naked on their back deck. It's July and so a hot night even for Calgary. It's her idea and more of a dare. *I'll do it if you will,* she'd said. Now they've done it.

He likes the feel of a light breeze on his bare skin. His eyes have adjusted enough that he can see her and as far as the back fence. But there's not moon tonight. He's made sure of that already. The sky is clear, and the stars are visible despite the lights from the city that are but distant glows beyond the back alley.

She slides her chair a bit closer to his and the noise of metal against wood on the deck sounds much louder in the dark.

This is cozy, she says and puts an arm around his shoulder. The heat of her warms him and he likes how that feels in the slight cool breeze that has now picked up.

Now what? he asks.

We sit here and enjoy it. When we were younger, we wouldn't have considered for a second doing this.

She's right about that so he doesn't answer. The third song of *Hair* plays now, and he's already decided that its boring and that after all these years he wonders what all the fuss had been about.

He lifts a hand to Dawn's breast and gently strokes it.

That feels nice, she says in that cooing voice he's come to love so much. She's lifted her arm from his shoulders and hunts in his pubic hairs until she finds him and strokes slowly.

Will feels himself become hard.

Lovely, she says and goes on stroking him.

He lowers his hand from her breast and searches around in her pubic hairs until he finds her moist. *Ooo,* she says in the deeper way he's grown to expect and like.

This was a good idea, she says, each word coming out slower as he is busy with his fingers, and she is too.

Let me, she says and gets up from her chair and sits on him sliding onto him and sits there. She doesn't move up and down although he can't help himself and thrusts several times.

Wait, she says.

By now a chorus is singing behind him and he's lost track of where in the album it is. He would like to turn it off as now the music is distracting but couldn't possibly stop now to do that.

It is then that he hears the helicopter. At first, he thinks it is part of the soundtrack as it is distant and vague in that way. Soon it's louder and more urgent. Then he sees the search light far to the north of them.

No, Jesus, Dawn says and at first all he can do is watch the odd progression of the search light as his middle feels so much pleasure from Dawn on top of him. She is moving now, slowly and she's leaned toward him so he can hear her building sighs in his ear. Her back is to the search light so she can't see any of it only hear the helicopter.

What is it? she asks.

Police helicopter, looking for someone. Really, she says.

All of this should make him go soft but being out here with Dawn on him makes him fall deep into himself and feels pleasure as far down as his toes. He's never felt it like that before.

The search light is only three blocks north now and the pilot is patiently advancing one street at a time. Who could they be looking for? Will the suspect come through their gate?

Dawn is moving faster now and her sighs closer together. It hasn't been this intense between them in years. He no longer is hearing the musical or even the helicopter. All he hears are her sighs and feels her rapid rhythm on top of him.

I'm riding you, she says now.

Yes, he says.

Does it feel good?

Lovely. Don't stop.

I won't. I'm riding you. Oo it is so lovely.

The search light is one block north now and the light sweeps from the east to the west in a slow pattern. Several times it stops as they examine something more closely below them.

So good. Sooo goooood. Dawn moans now and moves even faster. She's never moved that fast in all the years they have been making love but being out here naked in the dark has stirred up something in her he doesn't want to interrupt or disturb.

The helicopter is nearly overhead now, and so noisy. She freezes then and squeezes him, and he feels himself climax.

Good. I can feel that, she says. Then *Jesus,* and she is off him and inside the house. The light is to the east of them now and the helicopter nearly overhead. He gets up too and goes inside. She is giggling on the floor just inside the sliding glass door. Will closes the door and the noise of the helicopter is immediately dulled. He watches the light scan across their deck now and stop on the two chairs. It stays of them for only a second and then moves farther west.

Wow, that was something, Dawn says, and then giggles more. *I feel your wet all inside me. I like that.*

She's never said anything like that before although she has often said she likes it when he comes inside her.

Hair has reached the second side now or what had been the second side when he listened to LPs but he's listening to it streamed on Apple Music.

She holds him close, and he holds her too and naked and sweaty like this they roll around on the carpet hugging each other and giggling.

Do you think they saw us? she asks later.

No

Good. What are the odds? Pretty low, he says.

I hope they catch whoever they are looking for, she says.

Me too, he says. She's never been this warm beside him and so frantic as she hasn't stayed still for long.

Did you come? he asks.

Many times, she says. Even in here despite all that light and noise.

But it sure was wacky. It sure was wacky.

Tale of Washing the Dishes

THE DISHES IN THE SINK WERE NEATLY STACKED AND THERE WERE large gaps between each tower. One pile consisted of plate and another of bowls. Between the towers he'd arranged the flatware with spoons on one side, forks and knives on the other. Even the large and small spoons he'd separated from each other. Larry ran a hand over them now careful not to knock over the towers. He didn't turn on the water yet but ran a bead of dish soup over the flatware and then up and down each tower. The dishes had been in the sink since this morning and now he was washing them. When he turned on the tap. he set the flow very light, so the thin stream of hot and cold water blended to lukewarm. He let the water flow and watched the soap form small yellow bubbles in the bottom that turned white the more water he added.

The bottom of the sink was covered now, and he watched the water slowly rise over the first layer of each tower. The spoons disappeared from view first and then the knives and forks and some of those were angled up and stuck out of the water like karsts he'd seen protruding from the ocean in beaches in the far east. But here the water continued to rise covering all but the sharply angled knife and fork. The towers were covered to four layers. All of the towers were white, ceramic as that was the only colour and type of dish they'd ever bought. He let his hands rest in the water and felt that warmth rise to his wrist. And still he waited.

He heard noises in the living room and knew what that meant but he didn't move from where he was. The window over the sink had a view of the back fence which was grey and high enough to hide the alley beyond it. He went out there four times a week to take out the garbage to the bins back there. The bins were plastic. Once they'd been tin or aluminum but were plastic now. They were same size as the metal ones but lighter when empty. He heard a car pass in the alley but couldn see it because of the fence was too high but he could tell it was a car and not a truck by the sound of the exhaust.

The water was now three inches above his wrist and the towers were nearly all covered by water. He lifted out his right hand and turned off the water. The kitchen was very quiet and so was the living room and the alley. This new quiet stopped him, and he returned his hand to the water and felt the grime swirl around both his hands. He should have made the water hotter as that was best for washing dishes, but he's always used lukewarm water. That came from his childhood when water was precious and rarely hot.

He heard her walk their sons upstairs. They will talk a lot up there, the boys fond of asking questions. Twins asked more than twice as many questions. Sky asked him this morning what coffins were made of. He didn't know Sky knew about coffins already as he'd never mentioned them and was certain that Sheila hadn't either.

Sky was the one who asked most of the questions and Josh usually listened to the answers and then asked follow-up questions.

Larry told Sky that coffins were made of wood. Josh had then asked, *why wood?* Larry hadn't had an answer for that, so he looked at his sons and all he could think to say was that *wood used to be cheap.*

Is it cheap now? Josh had asked back.

Larry had said that wood wasn't cheap now ,but people were used to coffins being made out of wood.

But if they were made of plastic, they would be lighter and stronger, Sky had said.

Larry didn't have an answer for that either and as he stood washing dishes now, he thought it wasn't such a bad idea except he couldn't really imagine how they'd be manufactured and transported.

They would look too plain. He'd said then.

Why would that matter if they're just buried in the ground? No one sees them once they are buried. Josh had said then.

He didn't know how his sons knew so much about coffins as no one in either his or Sheila's immediate family had died yet. Nor had his sons ever been to a funeral. He didn't tell them how the wood breaks down with the soil and it all gets mixed in over time, and plastic would take centuries to break down. But then people had once buried the dead in stone tombs so what was the difference?

He'd changed the subject then telling them about the weather in Paris as that was the first thing that popped into his head.

He pushed those thoughts aside now and raised his right hand out of the water and gripped the dish brush on the left side of the sink and put it in the water. He then took the top plate from its tower and submersed it in the water and rubbed the brush over both sides of the plate and then lifted the plate out of the water and rinsed it under stream of cold water in the other sink. He then set it in the plastic tray to the left of the main sink. That tray was red, and they'd bought it at the hardware store a month ago. *A red tray.* He'd thought and knew immediately that he'd liked that idea and still did.

He now took a bowl from the top of the bowl tower and repeated what he did with the plate and only turning on the stream of cold water in the other sink when the bowl was completely clean and ready to be rinsed.

When both towers were below the surface of the water Sheila came into the kitchen and hugged him from behind and asked if he wanted help. He said that he was fine and was nearly finished. He asked how the boys had been, and she said they'd been a little excited but were asleep now.

What did they ask about? he asked her.

She doesn't answer right away and then said that Sky had asked why grass is green.

What did you say?

I couldn't think of anything at first because how do you answer that?

She was right, *how do you answer that?*

Finally, I said because it's not blue. Sky pinched his face then and his eyes narrowed to slits and Josh did the same and for a second they were mirror images of each other. Josh said then that the sky was blue and so was water. I said that water only looks blue from a distance and that in fact water is clear and not blue at all. And so is the sky I said. Has everything always been coloured that way? Sky asked. I said as far as I knew. Okay Josh said and Sky didn't say anything for a long time. Then he asked me to tell them a story and I did.

He didn't ask her right away what story she'd told them but instead raised the dish brush out of the water and saw how grimy it was so he put it back in the water and shook it several times and then raised it out of the water again and this time it was all clean so he used it to wipe the remaining dishes. The water in the sink was much lower by then and filthy. The flatware was visible. He took out the plug and when all the water was gone, he put the plug back in and half-filled the sink with water. By now she'd dried off some of the plates and bowls and put them away.

What story did you tell them? he asked.

The one about the girl and the slide. You haven't told them that one before.

No, I was saving it. Tonight, seemed like the right time to tell it. Did they ask any questions about it?

Not one. By the time I was finished they both had their eyes closed already.

He'd always like that story since she told it to him when they were first dating. It didn't take much for him to guess that she was the girl in the story and that the slide had been the one that was still in the back yard at her parent's place. Their sons had gone down that slide many times.

The fact that she'd told them that story tonight meant there was going to be much happiness in the days ahead. He quickly cleaned each piece of flatware with the brush and then rinsed those one at time and set them in the tray. She didn't dry those or put them away but left them in the tray.

She sat at the round table near the sink. When he was finished, he drained the left sink and wiped it with the same brush and then thoroughly rinsed the brush under the tap and then set it to dry on the left edge of the red tray and away from the flatware.

He'd get the boys to help put them away in the morning. They liked doing chores like that. Sky liked to put away the knives and forks and Josh liked to put away the different sized spoons. When they were finished, Sky liked to clap his hands twice while Josh watched.

Now that he'd finished washing dishes, he joined Sheila at the table. She looked at him and smiled.

The girl and the slide. That's a good story, he said.

Yes, she said. *But I can only tell that once,* she said.

He agreed. Some stories were like that. For some reason in that moment, he thought about the dish brush and the service it had just done and how every day it served the same purpose. *Now that's a story,* he thought but didn't share that thought with Sheila. Instead, he glanced in the direction of the red tray but couldn't see the brush from this angle. Could only see the flatware sticking up from their plastic pockets. *Plastic coffins* he thought then. *What an idea.*

Tale of the Thai Cat

SHE WAS A STRAY WHO'D COME INTO HIS YARD MONTHS AGO AND stayed. Mostly she was a nuisance and mostly underfoot at inopportune times. She'd tripped him up a couple of times and once he'd landed hard on both hands and then his knees. Aom had scrapes on this knees and hands for weeks from that. But those had healed now, and he'd adjusted to the cat being around and adopted her but didn't give her a name or ever call her as she was always around. Every day, he left out scraps for her from his evening meal. He'd scrape what was left on his plate onto the concrete floor just outside the kitchen door. The cat would never be in sight when he did this but not long after she'd hurry from out of nowhere and gobble it up.

He'd set out a bowl half full of water too and that would be empty by morning although he'd never see her drink from it.

For a year Aom adjusted to the cat being around and she'd adjusted to his daily habits. She'd seemed a scrawny but healthy cat.

Whatever her life had been like before she'd wandered into his yard, he didn't know except for the signs it had left on her. She'd been scrawny and easily spooked and her fur had been mangy. It was clear to him that she'd been neglected. She fattened over the past year but not by much. The scraps he'd given her likely weren't enough, but they were all he could spare. He ate sparingly himself usually sticking to two meals a day: a light breakfast and a more substantial meal in the evenings. For a great stretch of each day, he felt hungry but that was part of his daily practice.

Aom had been retired more than a decade and his pension was so meagre it barely covered his monthly food costs let alone anything else. His life had never been one of extravagance or luxury. It had been a life of worship, study, and belief. Because of that he knew the cat hadn't appeared by accident because there were no accidents.

The cat would disappear for large portions of each day. He had no idea where she went. He did look for her several times searching various hiding places around his property where he imagined a cat would hide but he never found her. He assumed that she found somewhere cool for the hot afternoons, but he never learned where that was.

Today she didn't appear when he scraped his leftovers onto the ground. He waited and even clanged his spoon and fork against his plate to let her know her food was ready. Still, she didn't appear.

He took his plate and cutlery back into the kitchen and closed the door and rinsed them under the sink and then washed them in soapy water and set them to dry in the plastic dish tray next to the sink. He assumed that by the time he was finished cleaning the dishes, she'd be eating the scraps, but when he opened the kitchen door to check on her, she wasn't there, and the scraps hadn't been touched. He called her quietly at first and then louder and then made loud cat noises. Those normally worked when everything else failed. But today after a half hour of this she still didn't appear.

Aom retrieved his wooden chair from the main room of his bamboo hut and brought it outside and sat in it and waited for her to appear. By now the sun was low in the sky and the day's heat nearly gone. The food tired him, and he fell asleep in the chair. As he slept, he kept having the sensation of being about to fall but caught himself each time. But then he didn't catch himself in time one time and woke on the ground next to the chair. It was dark out, so he felt ahead until he reached the chair again and used it to help him stand. He then walked to the kitchen and turned on the single bulb outside light and then the light over the sink and left the door open so that light spilled outside to where the scraps still lay untouched on the ground. He called again for the cat and walked around his small yard as he did so. He went as far as the front gate and then to the back wall and then to the east wall and back to his hut. Aom did this five times, but the cat didn't appear.

He wondered then if she had run away or found a better place to live. But after her being here for more than a year and her advanced age, he suspected that something had happened to her. He had no idea what that was or where she might be. At this moment, Aom didn't know if he would see her again. He sat in the chair facing the scraps and meditated. As he did, he saw many cats in his mind. Cats from when he was a boy. Cats he'd seen in the street. Cats that only existed in his imagination. Those cats were large, small, old, or young. They were calico cats like the one missing, or black and white, or grey, or brown cats. Some slept and some meowed and others rolled around on the ground. He didn't break his meditation but went deeper and became a cat and the first thing he noticed with his cat vision was that all the colours were gone and all he saw were shades of white and black. He saw the scraps on the ground and smelled them but felt no appetite for them. He meowed several times and each meow meant something different, and he sensed those difference but not as words but as a deeper sensation than words. A pure sensation of being.

When he came out of that mediation, he could see that the scraps still hadn't been touched. His legs and arms were stiff and sore, and he rose slowly from the chair and carried it into the house and set it back in its corner of the room. He checked once more on the food and then closed the door and went to his small cot and laid down and was soon asleep. He slept through the night and when he woke, he had to pee badly so peed into the pot he kept under his cot for that purpose. He then carried that out to the small herb garden he had near the east wall and poured his pee over it to help everything to grow faster.

He carried the empty pot back to the kitchen, and as he passed the scraps, he noticed that some of them were gone but most of them remained. He rinsed the pot under the tap for a long time and then set it out in the sun to dry. He stopped back at the food and determined that, so little had been eaten that more likely a rat or mouse had eaten there during the night. He looked around the yard and called but didn't see the cat. He went inside and prepared his usual meagre breakfast of sticky rice and flakes of tuna. He ate that slowly chewing each mouthful until there was no flavor left and then swallowed. He set aside a couple of tablespoons of tuna for the cat and two thumb size chunks of rice. He then scrapped those onto the ground next to the leftovers from yesterday. He called to the cat and waited but she didn't appear.

Aom went inside and sat in the lotus position next to his cot and did his morning chants and meditation. This time when he meditated, he saw many animals but none of them were cats. He saw rats and elephants and monkeys and tigers and spiders and geckos but no cats. Some of the animals could talk like the elephants and monkeys but the others were silent and simply moved away from him. He followed them, but they hurried away and were soon not there at all.

When he came out of this meditation, the hut was already stuffy with heat, and he knew that meant it was noon and that he'd been meditating for several hours. He washed his hands and then went outside, and all of the tuna and rice were gone but the leftovers from yesterday hadn't been touched. He called for the cat, but she didn't appear. He wasn't certain she had been the one that had eaten the food. When he was near the east wall, he saw movement in the tall grass there and knew that meant a rat. He hurried in that direction and saw a long tail disappear through a hole at the base of the cement wall. He should plug that up, but it was one of the ways the cat came and went.

That evening he chopped green papaya and tomato and made papaya salad. He also dished out the remaining flakes of tuna from the can and saved a larger portion than usual of for the cat. He scraped this into a fresh corner so he could easily note when it had been eaten. He swept up the other leftovers with a broom and put those in the garbage can in the kitchen. He brought out his chair and waited for the cat, but she didn't appear. After dark he called her for over an hour until his throat got sore. Aom carried his chair inside early and meditated on the floor next to his cot.

This time he was able to fully empty his mind so not a single image or sound came to him and soon he floated away and soon became a continuous drifting without a destination. He didn't break from this drifting until it was very late. When he opened his eyes and was back in his hut, he slowly unfolded his legs, and they were so sore it took him a long time to stand. When he checked the time, it was the middle of the night.

He opened the kitchen door but none of the scraps on the ground had been touched. He closed the door and peed in his bathroom and laid on his cot and was soon asleep. He woke later than usual in the morning. He'd dreamt that he was swimming in a cool lake and the land around the lake was flat and treeless. He had the sensation of needing to pee and tried to pee in the lake but couldn't. This woke him and he immediately rose and peed in the pot from under the bed and carried it outside and deposited the contents in a different part of his garden. When he returned to the kitchen, he saw that all of the tuna and salad were gone. Only a couple of dried strips of papaya remained. This gave him hope. He called for the cat more loudly than before, certain that she had to be nearby, but she didn't appear.

What could possibly have happened? he wondered. Had the cat even eaten the food, or had it been the rat he saw yesterday? That thought darkened his mood. He considered not putting out any more food because if all he was doing was fattening up a rat, that wasn't wise.

He went inside and prepared a breakfast of a single boiled egg, sticky rice and two slices of apple. He ate both slices of apple but left some of the egg and rice. Her favorites were egg and rice. So he left her a good portion of each and scraped those onto the cement outside the door. She didn't appear as she usually did but he was used to this by now so went back inside to do his morning chanting and meditation. When Aom finished and came outside all the eggs were gone and most of the rice. It looked as though she had just been here and he called her again circling his yard as he did so. The sun was blistering hot by now and tired him easily and so went back into the shade of his hut. He left the door open so that it could cool a bit.

He sat on the floor and closed his eyes but didn't meditate. He simply rested there in the dark of his own head and was free of thoughts and by now was used to how elusive thoughts could be and how quickly they flitted by as though powered by something beyond his own mind. When he'd been younger, he'd been able to hold a single thought for hours at a time and explore all dimensions of that thought and learned that even a single thought could be extensive. Now he'd come to think of thoughts as a nuisance of the mind and something to become free of. He'd practiced this enough that now thoughts hardly existed at all and were little more than random flashes that appeared and disappeared without him registering them. At the very deepest realization of all this, he opened his eyes, and the cat sat a mere three feet from him, and her head was tilted to one side as though she were studying him.

She'd never come inside his hut before. He'd left his door open often and even called to her from inside, but she'd never ventured in. He'd assumed that was her habit and came from whatever life she'd lived before finding her way to him. It was because of that, at first, he took her presence here as mere illusion. But when he sat up a little, she sat up too. It was then that he noticed that her hip had been injured and when she moved, she favoured it. He stood then and started toward her, but she crawled away from him using her front legs at first and then she managed to pull herself up unto her back legs but moved very slowly because of it. He could have easily caught up to her but let her get away from him. Once outside she disappeared into the grass. He could see the top of her head from the doorway, but he didn't go after her.

There was nothing he could do for her he knew already. He had no sense of how long she could manage like this. Aom could catch her although that would cause her much pain. He could then take her to vet a few blocks away and the vet would say because of her age she would best be put to sleep. His meditation had told him not to do that. Instead, he knew he would go on putting out food for her and sometime during the night she would find her way to it and eat as best she could. He also knew that at some point she would stop coming for the food. He wouldn't find her then and would sense she'd crawled her through that hole in the wall and found a place to die. At that moment the leftovers wouldn't be touched again no matter how may days he put them out. In time he would stop and that would be the end of it.

His other routines would remain the same, but the cat would no longer be a part of it would no longer be underfoot to trip him.

He won't attach meaning to this or summarize it in any way just he never gave the cat a name. It didn't need a name or anything like that from him. The food she needed and a place to be and in that she was no different than any other animal including him. He will not dream about her or see her when he meditated. He will chant for her soul and help as best he can in helping it to go where it needed to go next.

Today, Aom prepared a larger evening meal than usual and put honey on the sticky rice and opened a fresh can of tuna and sliced up a tomato from his garden. He ate less than half of that and scrapped the rest onto the ground outside the hut. He stayed inside even though the waning day was still hot. To cope with that, he slowed his breathing and became detached from this hut and drifted toward the river a few miles east of here. He nearly made it there before he attached to his physical self again and sank into the deep inner heat of the hut. He got up slowly and went to the kitchen door and noticed that all the scraps were gone. He didn't call out for the cat but stayed in the open doorway for a moment caught between two kinds of heat. Aom eventually went for his chair and carried it to the tamarind tree near the east wall and sat there. *These are my days* he thought and then closed his eyes and listened for any sound that the cat might make but he didn't hear any he could claim came from her.

Tale of the Twins

A DRY DESERT WIND BILLOWS THE STREET WITH DUST. THEY STAY IN the car parked on the main street of the town. Betty wants her sister to keep driving to Flagstaff, but her twin sister has said that she's driven as far as she plans to for today. They sit side-by-side in the car with the engine off. Betty watches in the side mirror as a cloud of dust comes toward them and then engulfs the car. By then it's too late to get out. Audrey grips the steering wheel and reaches once to the ignition as though to start the Honda but doesn't. They left Phoenix late this afternoon bound for Flagstaff.

They left Vancouver two months ago and drove to Toronto and then into the US and then to New York City. From there they've driven south down the east coast and then turned west at Jacksonville and eventually on to Phoenix. From Phoenix they plan to go north all the way back to Canada and then west to Vancouver.

There hasn't been any wind until today. This trip is in celebration of their 70th birthdays. They've both been widows for a decade Their husbands died a month apart.

It's like that with twins. Events happen close together. Someone has said but Betty no longer remembers who.

The drive from Vancouver to Toronto has been long and the August heat has made her thankful for the Honda's air conditioning. They've listened to books on tape the whole way so far. Mostly to the novels of Anne Tyler. They started with *If Morning Ever Comes* and have worked up to *Saint Maybe* which finished playing this afternoon and they're about to start *Ladder of Years*.

Audrey put all of these on a thumb drive before making the trip having bought the audio books a long time ago. They'd both read *If Morning Ever Comes* when they were first married. Betty read it first and then loaned it to Audrey. They both loved it. Their tastes were twin tastes and Betty is convinced that even if they had grown up in separate households, they'd have both loved the writing of Anne Tyler amongst a whole host of other loves. Every time Betty has discovered that she has a particular liking for something she's soon discovered either that her sister already has that liking too or takes to right after as passionately as she does.

Betty's the instigator and Audrey the capitulator or so Betty has come to believe before this trip. But now it seems that those traits have reversed. Perhaps they'd always been this way and she's only now accepted it.

Audrey has done all the driving from Vancouver to here even though the Honda is Betty's. She and Herb bought it two years before he died, and she's only put few miles on it since. Even though it's over a decade old it still rides like new.

Before setting out, Betty had assumed that they would see a lot of wildlife in the drive across Canada especially through Kenora and northwestern Ontario, right through until Sault Ste Marie. But all they've seen is one moose and the tail of a fox as it hurried into the trees. They plan to stop in Flagstaff for the night, but both have agreed not to go to the Grand Canyon. Betty and Herb had gone there on a holiday in their fifties and Audrey went there with Gus when their children were young. All of them hiked along the canyon floor next to the river and took lots of pictures back when pictures were taken on film.

Betty saw Audrey and Gus's pictures only once not long after that trip when Audrey brought them over to show Herb and her. Betty had been amazed at how dark each picture was as though they were all taken in the shadows. In one Audrey was holding the hands of both her children. Gus had taken that picture and it wasn't as dark as the others. All three of them were smiling and looked directly into the camera. That's the one she remembers now and how the rust-coloured rock behind them had made them appear happier than their smiles did.

The cloud of dust has past and Audrey opens her door and gets out. She leans back into the car and says, *Are you coming?*

In a bit, Betty says.

Suit yourself, Audrey says and walks up the Main Street of the town.

Betty isn't certain the name of the town but knows it is less than halfway to Flagstaff and built where there are few trees and a lot of hills and sandy earth.

Audrey stops to look in the window of several shops. Betty could close her eyes and still sense every single shop that her sister will stop and look into. She might even be able to see what her sister sees although Audrey would poo poo such notions and say that she is just showing off or making stuff up. She does close her eyes now but draws a blank beyond her own dark head. The thoughts that do come to her are memories from when Herb and she visited the Grand Canyon. He'd been very healthy then and a much faster walker than her and she had to keep asking him to slow down and he always made such a fuss of it saying that walking fast was a way to stay healthy. But she's the one still alive not Herb. She doesn't take pride in that notion though and in fact it makes her miss him terribly so, more than she has in five years. She thinks about him often enough but he's part of her past now except for the memories that appear now and then without beckoning on her part.

Audrey and she haven't once talked about Gus or Herb on this trip. Even through all those Anne Tyler novels and all those odd relationships in them not once has the topic come up. She's thought about Herb every now and then like she does now, and she's assumed to that Audrey has thought about Gus in the same way, but they've mostly talked out all that past by now so it's where they are now that matters.

Audrey has stopped in front of a bookstore five stores down. She's moved close to the window likely to take in the window display. Betty knows that she'll go inside soon as it's impossible for her sister to pass up a bookstore. *I never get tired of reading* she's told Betty and Betty claims the same. Whatever books Audrey settles on this time Betty is certain she will like them too. This is more of Audrey being the instigator.

After Audrey goes into the bookstore, Betty gets out of the car and walks in that direction. She stops to take in each store window along the way even those her sister didn't stop at. The first store is a travel agency with pictures of mostly tropical scenes except for one in the top right corner that advertises a sailing to Antarctica.

The few pictures there have snow and ice in them. That would be the one she'd choose to go on, but she doesn't like tours. This trip with Audrey is as close as she'll ever get to going on a tour.

The next window is the *North Star Café*. She can see through the windows that it mostly has booths and one-half circle counter with stools. It's a lot like the cafes Audrey and she hung out at as teens on Main Street in Vancouver. Betty had been the talkative one then and Audrey the silent one. That had surprised people because they always assume that identical twins were exactly alike, but they're not. Their appearance might be the same, but on the inside, they were very different people.

The café is mostly empty despite it being near dinner time. A large man sits at the counter, and he is talking to a server there who is leaning a bit toward him. She assumes from the posture of both that they've known each other a long time and that the large man is the one who does most of the talking. Herb talked a lot and sometimes she'd have to shush him. He didn't take that very well and would sulk for a time, but when he came around, he'd always thank her because he didn't like talking so much but sometimes his mouth just took over, he'd say.

A man comes out of the café now. He's about Herb's age except much thinner and completely bald.

Going in?

No, she says.

Too bad the food's really good. I have the steak sandwich every time I can and that's often.

That's good to know, she says to him to be polite. She doesn't eat steak and mostly doesn't eat meat except fish and chicken, and she knows that's not technically meat as Herb had said to her many times.

I saw your sister earlier. I haven't seen that many twins, but I like how different you dress.

Audrey is wearing a blouse and skirt and Betty is wearing blue jeans and a checkered shirt. At least he doesn't say she looks like a man as she's tired of hearing that. This style suits her, and Herb always said it looked sharp on her, so she hasn't varied from it.

Passing through?

Yes. She knows by now that his coming outside just now isn't by accident. Maybe at first, he thought his vision was going bad seeing the same woman twice looking in the front window but the difference in clothes must have tipped him off.

I'm going that way, she says pointing in the direction of the bookstore.

Right, McArthur's Books. That's been there a long time. William McArthur used to own it, but nobody named McArthur owns it now, but everyone in town knows it by that name so it's stuck.

She wonders how he'd know that is where she is headed but then decides that tourists must always end up there.

I like to read too. Got that from my late sister. She liked to read Anne Tyler novels. I read a few but they weren't to my liking.

Something was always off kilter in those books. The characters were always a bit too strange for my liking. My late wife read every one of them right up until she died a few years back. I assume there has been at least one or two since then, but I've never checked.

Two in fact, she says having worked out when his wife died.

Right, he says. *You like to read her books too then?*

My sister and I—

Ah right twins.

It's not like that. She detests now that he's come to that conclusion and wishes to be away from him. She thanks him for the tip on the café and turns away from him and toward the bookstore. She half expects him to follow as she's struck him as the lonely type that is eager to latch on, but he stays where he is. She senses his eyes on her.

At the bookstore she stops at the door and looks back in his direction. He still hasn't moved and waves to her. She waves back and then pushes open the door and it chimes as she steps inside.

She sees Audrey at the very back at the store holding a book. She turns at the sound of the door chime and looks in Betty's direction. Betty thinks she nods at her but she's too far back in in the store and it's not well enough lit there for her to be sure. She continues in and hopes that the man is gone by the time she and Audrey come out. She's never gotten the man's name and he's never gotten hers and she prefers it that way. Although she can't help but think about how her wife must have come in here often when she was still alive and maybe even ordered the Anne Tyler books as soon as they came out. Unlike her husband, she must have liked that parts that were off kilter and odd and maybe it was those things that she'd been craving in her life.

Those weren't the reasons that Betty liked Anne Tyler's novels and why her sister liked them too. It was how real they were and from time to time she'd recognize herself in them and from time to time even had similar thoughts as the characters in the novel. If Anne Tyler were here right now, she didn't know what she would say to her or ask her and suspects that she wouldn't even approach her at all but simply look in her direction and think *oh there's Anne Tyler,* and then continue browsing.

Tale of the Faithful Couple

SHE PARKS IN FRONT OF THE SAFEWAY IN TOWN. SHE'S BEEN BUYING groceries here since she married Dennis three decades ago. He worked in the papermill then and did so until his accident and then worked for the town. Shoveling mostly and in winter huddling in the office as much as possible. He took to paperwork in time. *It's just numbers,* he would say.

It had been agreed upon a long time ago that she would do the grocery shopping. She'd has her own career as an accountant for the Government of Ontario. Still as agreed once a week she drives to town from Longbow Lake. Now they have the same day off, but she still does the grocery shopping.

The drive into town takes her past many lakes whose views she's so used to by now so she only glances at them quickly to see if anything is different but it never is. That gives her great satisfaction. Much of the world seems sped up but out at Longbow Lake the days turn slowly. In the years she's been driving to town the traffic has gotten sparser and sparser. She'd grown up in town while Dennis grew up at Longbow Lake and he bought five acres near his parent's farm. Right on Longbow Lake. He still likes to fish. They have an eighteen-foot Lund with a ten horsepower Evinrude on the back of it. That's where Dennis is now. Out on the lake fishing for pickerel.

He'd been skinny in high school, but she'd noticed him all the same because he had the kind of face that would stay handsome and has. He's older-man handsome now but that's okay. He's not so thin anymore. He doesn't drink alcohol or smoke, so he has that in his favour.

She gets out of the Honda Accord. It's only a year old and their tenth car. Dennis and she had laughed about that when they bought it. Paid in full not on payments like lots of people do these days.

She goes to where the carts are lined up near the entrance to the store and takes the first one and pushes it through the electric doors. They open so fast that it's like they were never there.

She's done this for decades, but each time she goes shopping she feels the same rush of happiness as she pushes the cart through the open doors. *Where does that come from?* She has asked herself from time to time but now has given up wondering about it. *It doesn't matter. It just is. A gift. A moment.*

When their sons Wendell and Frank were young, she'd set them in the cart and arrange the groceries around them. They've grown up and moved to Winnipeg. Dennis and she drive up there on weekends to visit. Dennis usually drives there because he likes to drive in the morning and has trouble driving at night, so she drives back. She has always had better night vision.

She goes down the meat aisle first as always. It is the aisle along the west wall. The store has had the same layout for decades. She'd feel lost if she shopped at the mall in town. Dennis has pointed out that she'd get used to it, but she sees no reason to change now.

Dennis's accident happened during the rainy but hot summer of 1982. It was her day off and she was shopping in this store when it happened. She didn't hear a thing until she got home with the groceries and started to put them away. Then the phone rang. She ignored it at first thinking it was one of her many friends wanting to talk, but it kept ringing. When she answered she didn't recognize the man's voice.

Joyce? The voice asked.

Yes.

This is Arnie. There's been an accident. Dennis is okay but he's at the hospital.

She thanked him and hung up. She put the rest of groceries away and then got into their Pontiac at the time and drove to the hospital. Arnie had told her so little she had no idea what to expect. The receptionist she knew from high school and had a very serious face unlike any she'd ever had in school. She told her that Dennis was on the second floor. When she entered his room, it had been so dark. All the lights were off, and the blinds all closed. Dennis had the room to himself. It was a large room, so in the dark, it took her a moment to find his bed.

Dennis? She called out.

I'm here, he said, and his voice came from the opposite direction than she'd expected.

She went in the direction of his voice and her eyes had adjusted to the dark by then and she saw his bed and that he was turned away from her.

Dennis? she said again.

He turned to toward her and he seemed slower than she was used to and she could tell he was doped up because of the pain.

Joyce? He said her voice as a question.

She wondered in that moment who else he would be expecting. The nurse maybe?

That's when she noticed the bandage on his left arm stopped just after the elbow and there wasn't anything after that. It took her a few minutes to register that the rest was gone. No hand.

He told her then that *the logs had gotten jammed. I almost got them free and then—* It sounded like he was apologizing to her for something bad he'd done.

She sat on his bed and said, *Oh Dennis,* but didn't have any more words than that. She didn't leave that room the rest of that day or night except to go down the hall to use the bathroom. He was in there for a full week, and she was there most of that time.

Sometimes she'd drive to the Safeway to buy ready-made sandwiches for two of them when he got tired of the hospital food. Arnie and some of his friends from work came by for short visits. None of them talked much and most of the time they sat there and looked at each other. She knew they had to be more talkative than that at work, but the hospital must have threw them off.

Arnie told him he'd be okay that the papermill would take care of everything because he'd been injured on the job. He never once talked about Dennis missing a hand and half his arm.

He acted as if Dennis would come back to work, but Dennis had already told Joyce that he had no intensions of ever going back to work there.

Still, he let Arnie go on talking as though he would be and never corrected Arnie and neither did Joyce.

At night she'd lay in the hospital bed beside him, and they'd talk in the dark. They'd keep all the lights off so the only light visible would be a thin glow from the hallway under the door. She'd hear people walking past and voices rising and falling but they all might as well be a million miles away for all she cared.

He'd been so chatty in the dark and she attributed that to whatever they'd given him for the pain. He said he couldn't bear the thought of going to work in the papermill again after what it had taken from him. She agreed understood the betrayal he felt and how unforgiveable it was especially because it had been a machine that had done it. She lay on his right side so she wouldn't bump his wounded arm. Then one night out of the blue he said, *I've always been faithful to you Joyce.*

That had surprised her then and she'd wondered what had prompted him to say it. She told him that she'd always been faithful to him too. This was perfectly true, and she fully believed that his statement had been perfectly true too.

She'd always believed in his fidelity and hadn't needed it confirmed but in that moment in the dark it had seemed important that they both confess that. If it could be called a confession.

That's a lovely thing, he'd said and then went very quiet, the medication having caused him to fall asleep. She listened to his breathing and how so perfectly regular it was, and she hoped that if he was dreaming that he was having a good dream and one where he still had both hands.

He woke her many hours later and he was kissing her cheek and his good hand stroked her neck. He'd often done that in the night when he was aroused and keen to make love. She liked being waken that way and the urge in her would be rapid and she didn't really understand her body in that moment and yet its eagerness and hunger pleased her, and she'd let her mind drift away.

He didn't attempt to make love then and seemed content to kiss and stroke her. She let him and then later she kissed and stroked his cheek. This seemed oddly more intimate than any other moment in their lives together. He was in the hospital for another week after that and nurses let her spend the nights there, but they never once were intimate like that again. On the day he checked out he kept going to use his left hand and then would catch himself and say *Oh*.

That was six years ago now and he's become very adept at having only one hand. He's never gotten a prosthetic even though his doctor has recommended it many times. He's said he doesn't want a foreign contraption attached to him. He's gotten very good at one- handed driving and fishing. She doesn't worry about him being out on the lake by himself as he's every bit as capable as he ever was. He wears a sock over the stub on his arm so as not to offend others. She likes the smoothed skin of the wound where it has healed and sometimes strokes it when they make love, but others have been taken aback. He always wears the sock now even when he is alone like now fishing.

She selects a full chicken for roasting and pork chops and two salmon steaks. They don't eat beef and haven't in a long time. Likely they will have fresh pickerel for dinner today so all of this will go in the freezer. She goes to the produce aisle next which is on the far side of the store. She will go to the bakery last. She doesn't buy many goods from the main aisles and often doesn't even venture into them. At the checkout, Wanda is ahead of her. They were in the same classes in high school and had talked often then but aren't close now.

How's Dennis doing?

He's out fishing right now.

Good

Most people she's not that close to like Wanda ask about Dennis first. Everyone in town knows about the accident and how it's turned out and it's the one thing they can think to ask about.

Say hi to him, Wanda says in a way that might have made Joyce jealous once but not now. Dennis had told her many years ago that he'd been friendly with Wanda when they were in high school.

He'd never said what that meant exactly, nor did she ask. Wanda has gained a lot of weight, but she smiles every bit as friendly as she did in high school and Joyce concludes that she's as happy as ever even though her body is so different.

That's how it is living in a small town like this. She keeps running into her past. Worse yet, the people she meets carry around different versions of that past from her own. Their memories of it are distorted differently from hers and over time all the pain of what has happened is gone and the rest made palatable like Dennis's accident. It is all just something to talk about to indicate that they remember it together, but they don't really. She and Dennis, like everyone else, carry their versions of the past around as though it were continuing to play out somewhere in the distance, and if they worked hard at it, they could make their way back to it. As though all of that ,even his accident, went on existing somewhere fully intact.

At the Honda Accord she opens the trunk and loads in the bags of groceries one at a time. The day of the accident she'd been as calm as she is now. The parking lot is mostly empty as it was that day. The Honda is much smaller than the Pontiac and she likes how easy it is to park and get around town. She drives a steady 60 mph all the way home. The Honda is lower to the ground and hugs the corners better than the Pontiac or any other car they've owned before and gets terrific gas mileage.

She puts the groceries away and sits in the breakfast nook that has a full view of Longbow Lake below the house. She watches as Dennis comes around the point and motors toward home. He has the boat going full out and then slows perfectly near the dock. She can see then that he is steering with the stub of his left arm and only uses his right hand to adjust the throttle. She's loved him since high school and does even more so now, even if he's a completely different person. She knows she's a different person too. Less patient. Less shy and stands up for herself in ways she didn't in high school. Then she was told to defer and to hold back.

Don't do that. Dennis had said to her at one point, and she found a way to stop being like that.

She hears him at the front door and when he's fully inside, he says *Look what I caught Sweetie?* He holds up at half dozen sizeable pickerel dangling from a line off metal stringers. He holds them up with the stub of his left arm. One fish at the very bottom flicks its tail.

I'll fry those up right away, she says.

Good, he says and smiles and sets the fish in the kitchen sink. There's the metal noise of the stringer scaping against the metal sink and then all is quiet. He comes to her and kisses her, and he smells of fish and the lake. He doesn't have the sock on his stub and it's bare there and she reaches a hand to it, and it is warm and damp.

Later, he sits across from her in the nook and sets both arms on the table and she takes his hand with one of hers and his stub with the other. This is all so familiar and normal now she looks only at him and he only at her.

Tale of the Recently Departed

HER GRANDFATHER DIED AND AS WAS THE CUSTOM IN HER COUNTRY she sat three nights for him. But on the third night she fell asleep in the chair and dreamt of her grandfather at the wheel of a large freighter. Her grandfather had never been to sea and had never been on board a freighter that she knew. He'd spent his entire life on land. Yet here he was steering this massive freighter in a severe storm. The waves were as tall as a five-story building and he kept the freighter facing straight into each wave and the freighter rode up it and down again and then up again and down. Water splashed over the bow each time the freighter rose into the next wave.

Here you take the wheel, her grandfather said in the dream.
Me?
Yes. It's time you tried it.

She stepped forward and he stepped to one side and gestured with a hand like a maître d' leading someone to a table. She gripped the wheel and immediately felt the full weight of the ship and the forces of the wind and waves outside. Until then she'd simply been riding and balancing herself where necessary as the ship leaned one way or another. The water looked menacing, and each wave was large and white capped. Straight ahead the sea was an undulating mix of grey and white for as far as she could see. She struggled with the wheel as the ship wanted to go one way and then the other. She held the ship as straight into the waves as her arms could manage. They ached and she felt painful spams in each starting at her wrists and travelling to her biceps.

The freighter took the second wave straight up and down and the steepness of the wave was so marked that for a brief time the ship felt weightless and then the front of the freighter rose again. The next wave was even steeper down and she was certain the ship would go straight to the bottom of the sea, but it didn't. Instead, it reared up in the next wave and she felt the power of the engines as they pushed with a force equal to the force of the sea. The ship vibrated beneath her feet, and she looked down briefly and saw that she was wearing red shoes, a colour she'd never worn.

When she looked up again, the freighter was angled to the left and the next wave caused it to lean way over and she heard things slide along the floor of the wheelhouse, but she didn't dare take her eyes off the sea. The ship slid down the next wave and was even more turned to the left and came up partly sideways in the next wave.

She knew given the power of the sea that the freighter would be toppled over in the next big wave. She struggled to get the ship turned more into the waves, but her arms weren't strong enough to turn the wheel that much.

Her grandfather then was at the wheel too and they were both fighting to get the ship angled straight into the waves again. It took significant effort from her and her grandfather, but they managed to get the ship pointed into the waves. She was panting by then but her grandfather wasn't breathing fast at all.

Try again, he said and stepped back and left her alone at the wheel. This time she had a better idea what to do and after the ship dropped into the next wave anticipated the push of the wind as she came up into the next wave and angled the ship a little to the right. This worked as the wind pushed the bow to the left just enough, so it took the next wave straight on.

You're getting the hang of it, her grandfather said. He was behind her somewhere and she couldn't see him without turning around and she wasn't about to do that. It was then late in the day and getting dark, but the sea wasn't any calmer. She knew she would be at this all night and hadn't a clue how she'd do it in the dark with just the ship's lights to guide her.

You will be fine. For years, others have done this in the dark and survived just fine and so will you. Every day somewhere in the world a freighter is fighting a sea just as savage as this one is now. Her grandfather seemed able to read her mind. But it was a dream she reminded herself. But it seemed longer and more real than any dream she'd ever had, and she sensed that she wouldn't be waking any time soon.

This is but one lesson, her grandfather said. *There are many. Many? Yes. That is why I am here.*

She wasn't close to her grandfather and hadn't spoken to him in years except at holidays. Then she would call him. He was a widower by then and lived alone and would always answer on the second or third ring as though he sat near the phone.

When you marry make sure wear red shoes like you are now. They are your power.

Okay, she said because this was a dream, and she could agree to everything.

Watch, he said, and she realized that she had closed her eyes and when she opened them the freighter was dropping down a very steep wave so deep that the bow disappeared in a large splash of water when it rose again. All of it without her doing more than holding onto the steering wheel. The ship climbed and climbed into an impossibly high wave. Then she was staring at pure sky, gunmetal grey in all directions.

You've got the hang of it now so carry on, her grandfather said.

She woke then in her parent's house. Her parents had gotten up from their chairs and she heard them somewhere in the house. Her father coughed in the way he had for years.

A dry throat cough, he'd said whenever she asked. It was her father's father who had died. Her grandfather who had grown rice since he was a young man and knew rice and not the sea.

She got up from her chair and went to the kitchen where her mother was putting together bags of candy for those who will come to the service.

She helped her mother but thought about the dream. She will never go to sea and certainly never drive a freighter especially in a storm. The dream was terrifying enough.

These other lessons. Will they be in dreams? She wondered as she filled a bag of candy. *It was a dream of the recently departed.*

Nothing more. She decided and that thought calmed her and she let her mind drift with the task she was doing. She picked a red candy then a blue and a yellow and put them in a bag. Each time she picked the same colours in the same order. Three to a bag. Nor more and no less.

Tale of the Accident

THE 1968 COUGAR CAME TO REST JUST SHY OF A SECOND ROCK CUT farther down the bank. Steam rose from under the crumpled hood. Roy was twenty-eight and had been driving too fast. He sat stunned behind the wheel and was whisked back to when he was ten and fishing on Longbow Lake with his father.

They were sitting at opposite ends of the power boat. Their lines were in the water, but they hadn't caught any fish yet.

Don't get too hung up the future as it is always too far away. The present is here and now and all you've got. You and I fishing that's the only present there is right now. Let that sink in. To belong. The present is about belonging. Make sure you belong.

His father then proceeded to tell him about the day he met Roy's mother and how smitten he'd been. Roy had thought then that no one uses the word *smitten* anymore but he didn't say that to his father. Instead, he watched his line bob undisturbed in the water and listened to his father and sensed that he needed to remember every word and that they would matter later. He didn't know how he knew that then he just did.

I had no sense then of you or this future or how happy I have been all the years in between. Love should take you by surprise. It should blindside you. There is no greater power no greater course to happiness than through love. My father never told me anything like this, but I am telling you.

Now in his Cougar crunched between rocks, he surfaced for a moment and registered steam coming from under the hood and realized he couldn't move. He didn't remember much since he got off work at the lumber mill hours ago. He did remember having a few beers with friends at the Delmore Hotel in Kenora. It was dark out now, but his headlights were still on and shone on the grey rock straight ahead. He was sitting upright but had a brief memory of the car rolling several times. There was granite rock on either side of the car. He was wedged in good.

How many years after that day on the lake was his father gone? *Four.* He knew that answer even in the fuzzy haze of this wreck. He wondered if he will be the one gone now. What about his son and wife, Elizabeth? His head swirled again, and he was back at his wedding day. His father wasn't there. Was already dead. His mother stood beside him. He thought of his father saying the word *smitten* all those years ago and realized how wrong he'd been about it then as he couldn't think of a better word then. Nor did he have words for how he felt in that moment except—*good* and *happy.* At this moment he wasn't the one saying his vows or receiving Elizabeth's. He was standing to one side watching all of the proceedings like an explorer who'd come to a new land and discovered a fully functioning society and needed to watch very closely to properly understand what was transpiring. On one hand it was completely familiar and on the other it was foreign and impossible. *Who was I that day?* He asked now.

But then he was back in the car and the headlights had gotten much dimmer. *How long was he out?* He tried to raise an arm to shut the headlights off. *Save the battery. But why?* It hurt so much to move his arm even an inch that he gave up. He tried the other arm, but that one didn't move at all. He blinked his eyes and turned his head from side to side and then decided he shouldn't do that just in case. He closed his eyes and his head swirled again.

He was between his parents in his father's half-ton. He watched his father repeatedly slide the floor gear shifter between gears. He wasn't not really sure at that time why his father was doing that but it seemed impressive. His mother had her arm around Roy. *Brace yourself,* his father said and then the truck leaned one way and then the other and then back the other way again.

That was close, his mother said. And then a long time later she said, *Thank you,* to his father.

His father didn't respond but shifted gears and the truck sped up.

This couldn't be a memory. This couldn't have happened. *That had to be imagined. But can such a thing be imagined?*

He heard a tapping on the window and then a voice said, *Are you alright?*

No, he said.

Hold on, the voice said. He felt the door being open despite the rocks on that said. Cool air rushed in. He opened his eyes, and he recognized the OPP uniform but not the face.

Your cars banged up pretty bad. Can you move?

No

The ambulance will be here soon. Is there anyone you want me to call?

My wife.

What's the number?

Wait a second, he said and then a few seconds later recalled the number.

I'll be right back.

He was going to say he couldn't move if he wanted too but his mind swirled again, and he was back on the boat with his father.

Here again, he said.

What does that mean? his father said and then, *You've got a bite. Reel it in. I'll get the net.*

He thought then this wasn't how it happened. He didn't catch any fish that day only his father did. This was made up. A dream.

No it's not, his father said. *This is exactly how it happened. Your memories were wrong before today, but they are corrected.*

You can say that? he asked his father.

Of course. Remember what I told you about the present. Even this one in the car wreck. This is more real than any future you can imagine. You belong. I can see that, and it makes me very happy.

You never talked like that. he said to his father.

Yes, I did. All the time. You were just a boy. Keep reeling in your line. You've nearly got the fish to the boat. It's a pickerel. A large one. Got it. His father raised the net high, and Roy saw that it was likely a five-pound pickerel. Very large. Larger than any he remembered catching.

You're lucky I saw you. I almost drove past but I saw your headlights down the bank otherwise I would have gone straight past. The police officer was back now. *Hear that siren. The ambulance is nearly here.*

He didn't hear it. He heard a loud ringing in his ears. But he took the officers word on the siren.

How is he? Another voice said. This one was a woman's.

It'll be tough getting him out, another voice said. This one was a man's voice.

Move the stretch closer, the woman said.

Alright.

We'll need your help, she said.

Okay the officer said. *I ran the plates. His name is Roy. Roy, can you hear me?* The woman asked.

Yes, he said.

Good we're going to move you slowly. Don't resist let us do the moving. But tell us if it hurts and we'll stop.

Okay.

His head swirled then, and he was sitting in this car outside the Delmore Hotel. He's had too much to drink, but he put the key in the ignition and started the Cougar. He loved the rumble of the engine even as it idled. He let it idle for a long time. He turned on the radio and *One of These Nights* by the Eagles was in the middle of playing and he turned that up so loud the car vibrated from the beat. If any other song had been playing, he might have turned the car off and gotten out and called a taxi, but that song sounded so good when the car was moving. He was headed out of town by the time the guitar solo kicked in.

Easy, the woman said, and he was back. He had the sensation that he is lying down now and no longer in the car but being carried. He felt his body being raised and then lowered.

Wait the man said and metal doors clanged open.

Ready? the woman asked, and two male voices said, *Yes.*

Roy opened his mouth to say yes but couldn't form the word. He was being slid into the ambulance. It smelled of rubbing alcohol and something else, gauze maybe or tape. He couldn't decide which.

You're lucky. It looks like an arm and a leg everything else seems fine.

Thank you, he said and then the ambulance was moving. Slowly at first and then he sensed it going faster. He heard the siren outside now and whenever they passed a rock cut it echoed into the ambulance.

It won't be long before we reach the hospital. I've seen much worse so in a day or two you'll be feeling much better.

Thank you, he said again. This time he was able to form the word and she must have heard him because she nodded.

Try to rest, she said.

He closed his eyes and smelled the inside of the ambulance even more. He swirled and was sitting in a hospital room. *You're father's dead now. But he was glad you were here,* his mother said.

This didn't happen. Yes, it did, his mother said. But his father died in Winnipeg and he and his mother were in Kenora.

This is exactly how it happened, his mother said.

No, he said and forced his eyes open. The woman paramedic was sitting close, and he could see her face. Her hair was short. He was sure he'd seen her around town somewhere.

We're here, she said and in that instant the ambulance stopped. A second later, the rear doors swung open, and he saw the OPP officer and two other paramedics and several orderlies from the hospital. The orderlies wore light blue uniforms the paramedics dark blue ones. The stretcher was rolled out of the ambulance and magically legs dropped from it, and he was pushed into the hospital.

What do we have here? a nurse in all white asked.

Car accident, the OPP officer said.

Right, the nurse said. *This way.*

He swirled again and he was back in the car, and the headlights swept abruptly from left to right. *Not the rock cut, not the rock cut,* he screamed aloud. Then everything went black, and he heard metal crunches and then several pops. Then the radio cut off and the engine chugged, sputtered and died. *Not the rock cut,* and then his father's voice, *there is only the present. Always the present.*

Even this is the present. The future is too far away.

Tale of the White Toyota Corolla

ROB WAS BEHIND JUNE IN TRAFFIC TODAY. HE HADN'T SEEN HER IN the five years since they broke up, but he recognized her white Toyota Corolla and shoulder length blonde hair. She'd had both when they were together. She taught grade two and he grade six and they taught at the same elementary school. That was where they met. Their romance had been hot at first and then it wasn't and by the end they both agreed they weren't in love and that was that. He's had two cars since then and was driving a navy Honda Fit now. He came up close enough behind her white Corolla to notice that she had dark highlights in her hair, something she hadn't had back then. He braked and slowed but stayed two car lengths behind. He wondered about the mole she'd had on the back of her right hand and if she'd had it removed by now but decided she likely hadn't. The mole was one of the things about her that had attracted him. Rob couldn't imagine being attracted to a mole now. Time had a way of changing what was important. He didn't teach anymore but worked in publishing. She'd always been the detailed one and he thought in terms of the big picture, so she was likely better suited to the editorial work he did. He was certain that she was still working as a teacher and her back seat was filled with grade two picture books. She drove faster than he remembered her driving back then. She'd always been the one to drive and said she preferred that, so he'd sat in the passenger seat of that Corolla any time they went somewhere together. At River Street she went straight but he turned right and continued to where he was going.

Sometimes one of the twins asked Marge what he was like back in those lost years before they were born, and Marge always said that he'd had lovely thick sideburns. He wondered what sideburns had to do with anything but knew not to ask.

Acknowledgements

THE FOLLOWING TALES HAVE PREVIOUS APPEARED IN THE FOLLOWING magazines and I wish to think the editors for being in these works.

Tale of Amber Eyes in *Edifying Fiction Christmas 2019 Issue Tale of the Letter* in *Grain Magazine: Volume 47, Number 2*

Tale of the Pink Puppet and *Tale of the Blue Bicycle* in the anthology, *This Will Only Take a Minute,* Guernica Editions.

I also wish to thank the BC Arts Council for their financial support toward the writing of these pieces.